Isabella

Kyana Buckett

Contents

Prologue

Prologue

Ashley bit down on her bottom lip nervously and looked over at the clock.

It was half past nine. Three hours haves passed since Dante should have been home.

She stood up from her seat and started fiddling with her fingers, staring out the window every few seconds.

Where is he? She thought as she listened for the sound of a car driving in. He has never been home this late before. He didn't even call.

Ashley knew that she sounded like a clingy wife right now but she couldn't help but worry for her husband's safety. He was never one to come home late but yet, three hours have passed and he still wasn't home.

She took her phone off the table and stared at the screen.

Zero new messages.

A small groan escaped her lips and she stared at the window, as if her husband was going to magically appear right before her. She sat down on the couch again and turned on the T.V. hoping that it would keep her mind occupied.

The sounds coming from the T.V. did nothing to cease her worry. Ashley felt her heart beating faster and faster as the seconds passed. She breathed in slowly to calm down her breathing knowing that being stressed out wasn't going to help out her situation one bit.

A small noise emitted from her phone and she snapped her head down. A disappointed sigh came out of her lips when she saw that it was only her mother-in-law, reminding her of tomorrow's gathering.

The nerves grew even more now that she remembered that tomorrow is Dante's twenty-fifth birthday.

She still haven't gotten Dante anything yet but she planned on giving him news that would change their lives forever. She looked down at her stomach and smiled.

Placing her hand on her belly, she gently whispered to it. "Hello my little darlings."

Dante knew that they were expecting but what he didn't know that they weren't just expecting one. They were expecting two babies.

Two miniature versions of either Dante or her.

She was hoping for a boy who looked exactly like Dante with a few traces of her in him. Dante also hoped it was a boy so that he could help his father protect their younger girls from possible suitors. She knew that he would be happy with either a boy or a girl though.

All that matters is that their babies come out healthy and happy.

She closed her eyes and dreamed about her babies.

The birth of them, their first word, first step, first birthday.

She thought of all the happy memories that she and Dante would make with their two beautiful babies. How Dante and her would teach their children to ride a bike for the first time, how they would teach their children various sports to teaching them how to clean and cook.

She knew that she shouldn't be thinking that far ahead but she thought about their children's graduation and their prom night. How Dante would stare down their daughter's date and how she would fuss over her son's tux.

She thought of how Dante and her will sit in the porch and watch their grand kids playing in the sand.

That would her happy ending. That's how she wanted their lives to live out.

A sound of screeching tires snapped Ashley's out of her thought and she moved the curtains to look out the window again.

A huge grin made its way to her face when she saw that it was her husband's Audi. She squealed lightly and opened the door up, waiting for him to reach the steps.

As he came closer to the light, Ashley frowned when she didn't see the happy-go going smile that was usually plastered on her husband's face no matter how rough the day was. As he came to her, she leaned in to kiss him but met his cheek instead.

Thinking nothing of it, she took his blazer and hung it up. Turning around, she almost bumped into Dante, who was staring at her with the coldest look ever.

"Dante? Are you feeling okay?" she asked worriedly, putting her hand to his forehead.

He looked at her and took her hand, pushing it away from him. It was gentle but at the same time, had an underlined roughness to it. Ashley felt hurt when he did that but she quickly covered it up and sent him a smile.

"I have some news for you," she said, smiling brighter.

"I have news for you too Ashley," Dante's business-like voice rang through her ears and she frowned. He have never used that voice on her before.

"Well, why don't we sit down and you—"

"I want a divorce." Dante stated calmly, looking her straight in the eyes.

Ashley's eyes widened and she felt her heart beating against her chest rapidly. "What? Dante what did you just say?"

"Did I stutter? I want a divorce Ashley." He repeated again.

As soon as those words came out of his mouth, Ashley knew that her life would never be the same ever again.

Chapter 1

C hapter 1

"Hi there. May I sit down?"

Ashley looked up from the book that she was reading and glanced at the man. Her eyes widened when she saw a handsome man standing in front of her.

With his dark hair and piercing grey eyes, he was a sight for sore eyes. His jaw was strong and slightly clenched while his lip was tugged upwards in a nervous smile.

She looked him up and down, biting down on her lip.

Ashley blushed as she looked up, seeing the knowing look on his face. She can't believe that she was caught checking him out.

She nodded her head quickly and hid her face behind her book. Ashley felt her stomach fill up with butterflies. She tried to focus on the book but it was hard to when a Greek god was sitting right in front of her.

"You know, you're being a little rude right now." She heard him saying as he took a seat across from her. He slammed his books down on the table making her jump slightly.

Ashley pushed her book down a bit and rolled her eyes at him before returning back to her book. She bit back a retort and tried to distract herself again.

"Did you not hear what I just said?" The man asked, annoyance lacing his voice.

Oh god. Even with an annoyed tone, he still sounds hot.

"Oh I heard." Ashley snipped back coolly with a small hint of a scowl. She read the first few lines of the chapter and sighed.

It was impossible for her to concentrate with him sitting there.

Her forehead became hot and she knew it was from his piercing gaze.

"Well, it would be polite if you would say something or even acknowledge me." He had a husky and deep voice.

It made Ashley's inside churn with unwanted desire and she did all that she could to not let that desire show in her eyes.

Ashley looked around the cafe. A frown marred at her face at the sight of the emptiness. She started questioning why on earth the man would sit near her when there were many other tables still available.

She turned back to the man and raised her eyebrows at him. "I didn't find a reason as to why I should acknowledge you let alone be nice to you. Now if you would excuse me, I would like to continue reading my book." She gave him a pointed look before returning back to her book.

"Harsh." He muttered. "Pride and Prejudice? You're into literature?"

Ashley groaned and glared at him over her book. "Yes. Do you have a problem with that?"

Though the man was good-looking, Ashley knew better than to associate with people like him. He had the whole playboy attitude and it would be troublesome to get involved.

"People like me? Now what do you mean by that, mia bella? Please, amuse me." he asked with amusement.

"A player." She replied coolly. "Someone who thinks he's above everyone else and who have no problems with breaking the hearts of many innocent and young girls."

She put her book down on the table and leaned back against her seat. She looked at him with a raised eyebrow.

He chuckled and then crossed his arm over his chest. "And how would you know that?" he picked up her book and flipped it around.

Ashley glared at him.

She didn't like it when other people touched her stuff without asking.

"I just do." She snapped before snatching her book back.

"Feisty." He said with a wink before leaning back against his seat. "Well, that isn't right mia bella. Ever heard of never judge a book by it's cover?"

God he's such an annoying idiot. She thought to herself.

She watched as he raised his arm up, signaling for the waitress. His muscles flexed as he did so and she bit down on her bottom lip.

A hot idiot.

"A hot idiot you say?" he asked her in amusement.

Ashley cursed at herself for saying it out loud. Great. Just great. Now he knows that she was checking him out. Lord why must she always say things out loud?

A light blush made its way to her face and she glared at him before picking up her bag. Placing the book inside, she stood up and placed a twenty dollar bill under her coffee cup.

Sending a last glare to the man, she walked out of the cafe and into the fresh Californian air.

.

.

.

Ashley felt her whole world crashing down when he said that. Her heart felt like it was going to break into a million pieces and she could feel her head becoming lighter. Her eyes burned with unshed tears and her hands shook.

She backed into the wall and placed her palm on it, praying that that was enough to hold her up. "Dante. What do you mean? W-why would you want a divorce?"

"I don't love you anymore." He said coldly. "You're nothing to me." His cold and piercing grey eyes stared deep into hers.

Ashley let the tears fall.

He doesn't love her anymore?

"I don't understand. Dante, our children." She said softly, subconsciously putting her hand over her belly. "They can't live in separate homes. Whatever I did wrong, please tell me so that I can fix it. Our children need both of their parents."

Dante raised an eyebrow up at her. "Children? What do you mean by children? You don't mean?" he asked coldly.

Ashley nodded her head. She grabbed his hand and placed it over her stomach. "Yes, Dante we're having twins. I found out earlier today."

He gave her a cold look and roughly took his hand away. "Don't touch me." He hissed out at her.

Ashley whimpered and she backed up against the wall again.

Dante glared at her and took off his tie. "As for them, you don't have to worry. I'll sign away my rights. I don't even know if they're truly mine or not." He said before walking away from her.

"Dante wait! I don't know what's going on! What bought this upon you?!" Ashley shouted after him with her tears falling down excessively.

He paused for a second in his step. "I think you know exactly what I mean." He said coldly again but there was no mistaking the crack that was in his voice. "I trusted you." He said softly before leaving the house, slamming the door behind him as he left.

Ashley's knees buckled down from beneath her and she fell down. Loud sobs escaped from her mouth as her tears fell down one after the other. She buried her head into her hands and screamed loudly. She felt nothing but pain in her heart as it broke into tiny shards.

"What did I do wrong?" she asked herself out loud. Her hands reached out and touched the base of her stomach. Her heart broke even more if that was even possible knowing that there was a strong possibility that they won't even have a father.

She pushed herself up from the ground and winced in pain. She rubbed her stomach and sighed in relief when it went away. Wiping her tears, she told herself to calm down. Hiccups left her mouth and she let out a few more tears.

Using the walls as support, she started walking up the stairs and into her and Dante's room. Opening the door, she felt her heart constricting with pain as his familiar smell filled her nostrils. She let out a small sob before walking over to her bed.

She laid down on Dante's side and grabbed his pillow tightly. Inhaling his smell, she relished in it, knowing that possibly, this is the last time she'll be ever to be in the comfort of him. Tears continued soaking his pillow and she buried her head into it, sobbing softly.

She closed her eyes and prayed. Prayed that this was all just a nightmare and that she would wake up the next morning in his arms. Prayed that today had never happened. God how she wish it never happened.

A ring of the phone drew her away. She took her phone from the bedside and wiped away her tears. Without seeing who it was, she picked it up and answered it. "Hello?" she tried to hide any evidence in her voice that she was crying.

"Ashley? Sweetheart?" the voice of her best friend spoke up. "Are you okay? You sound like you were crying."

She felt herself tearing up again as she heard the words.

Never in her life has she hated the phrase 'are you okay' more than she did then.

"Mayla," her voice cracked and she clutched the phone tightly. Her eyes closed and tears continued to fall down.

They were endless and relentless. No matter how much Ashley willed they to stop, they wouldn't.

"Ashley what happened? Did you tell Dante the news?" Mayla asked her in a worried tone. "Did he not take it well?"

"I told him" she said quietly, "but."

"But what? What happened?" Mayla pressed on.

She wiped away her tears and took a deep breath. "Mayla, he wants a divorce."

There was a long pause at the other end. It was silent for about five minutes before Mayla spoke up again. "What are you going to do sweetheart?"

Ashley opened her eyes and stared at her wedding picture. She clutched the bed sheets tightly as she knew what she said next would impact her future for the rest of her life. "What is there to do Mayla? I'm going to give it to him.

.

.

.

Ashley woke up the next morning with a pounding headache. She groaned and clutched her head, sitting up on the bed. She looked over to Dante's side and frowned when she didn't see him laying there like he usually was.

Looking at the time, she frowned when she saw just how early it was.

He was never up this early. And if he was, he would always wait for her to wake up before doing anything else. So where was he?

She stood up from her bed and walked into the bathroom. Looking into the mirror, she cringed when she saw her red blood shot eyes and dark circles.

How did that happen?

Sighing, she started washing her face. Taking her toothbrush, she started brushing her teeth while rubbing her stomach with her other hand.

When she was done, she patted her face dry and walked into her closet. She put on some of Dante's sweats and one his t-shirts before walking down to the kitchen. "Dante?" she shouted out.

When she got no reply, she frowned and walked into the kitchen. When she didn't see him, she felt worry stirring in the pit of her stomach. She sat down on the table and grabbed the home phone. She quickly dialed his number and waited for him to pick up.

When it went straight to voice-mail, she frowned and placed the phone on the table. Putting her head into her hands, she prayed that wherever he is, he was safe.

When she removed her hands, she saw a white envelope sticking up from where the napkins were supposed to be. Curiosity took over her and she took the envelope. She grabbed the contents that was inside and she felt her whole body froze.

Legal Separation of Marriage.

The memories of last night flooded her brain and she felt the tears falling down again. Her vision blurred and her hands shook as she read through the divorce papers. She put her fist on her mouth to muffle her sobs. He had done everything. Had signed everything.

The only thing that was left was her signature on both the divorce papers and the custody. She snapped her eyes shut and prayed that this was just a dream. She pinched herself and cried even more when she realized that this wasn't a dream.

This was reality.

She looked to the side and saw a pen next to the napkin holder. Her hands reached out and took it. Ashley looked down at the papers again and did the only thing that she could do right at that moment.

She signed the papers.

Chapter 2

C hapter 2

Ashley was taking a sip of her coffee when she felt a shadow looming over her. She grew curious and looked up, instantly rolling her eyes when she saw exactly who it was.

"It's just you." She said dryly before removing her eyes away from him.

"Just me? Mia bella you wound me." He took the seat across from her. "It's nice to see you here. Such a coincidence, wouldn't you say? Some would even call it fate."

Ashley looked back at him and rolled her eyes when she saw his grin. "I beg to differ. On the contrary, I'm beginning to think that you're stalking me." She said before turning away again, refusing to look at the infuriating man.

This had been the third time she saw him today and every time, he would always try to spark up conversation despite her trying to ignore him.

The man seems to not be able to take a hint.

"Stalking you? Well mia bella I would never. But of course, how can I deny trying to get to know someone as beautiful as you?" his voice was filled with amusement as he answered her and that only seemed to infuriate her even more.

"Flattery will get you nowhere with me." She said dryly, turning to look at him again. She raised her eyebrow at him. "Now don't you have anything better to do than talking to me and infuriating me to no end?"

"Ah you're a feisty one. I like that." he smirked at her and in turn, she scowled at him. Chuckling, he answered her question. "There is something better that I would like to do right now."

"Then go and do it." She hissed out at him, picking up her cup of coffee.

"I would but then again, it all depends on the person who I want to do it with." He replied, staring straight at her.

Ashley took a sip of her coffee again and turned back to him, only to see him staring intensely at her. "Then go ask that person and leave me alone. I don't have time to deal with you."

He chuckled and shrugged his shoulders, leaning back against the seat. "Would you like to go take a walk with me? I would like to get to know you better."

"My nonna told me to never go with strangers." She replied sharply, letting some of her Italian accent seep through her voice.

"Nonna? And is that an Italian accent I hear? You're Italian?" he asked her with curiosity.

"My father is an Italian man. My mother was an American. I was raised in Italy for ten years before I left." She said, not deterring her eyes from her coffee cup.

"Why did you leave?"

"My father remarried. He didn't treat me the same after that. I asked to go live with my maternal grandparents and he didn't hesitate to ship me away." she replied softly, shocking herself at how much she had revealed to him.

"And your mother?" he asked in a soft and gentle voice.

Ashley gave him a fake smile before turning away again. She stared out the window. "She died giving birth to me."

It was silent for a few moments before he spoke up. "This is good."

Ashley snapped her head towards him and glared. "The death of my mother was good?"

His eyes widened and he quickly shook his head. "No I didn't mean good about that part. Your mother dying isn't something good."

"What is good about what I just told you then?" she snapped, continuing to glare at him.

"You're opening up to me. More than I actually expected." He smiled genuinely at her.

Ashley had to admit that his smile is one of the best smiles that she had ever seen.

Her face softened and she smiled lightly. "Well I guess." She sighed and looked in his eyes. "Why are you talking to me when there's a billion other girls out there who are way more prettier than I am? Why not waste your time on them?"

He leaned forward and gave her a strange look. "Because you're not like other girls. You intrigue me. I'm not wasting my time but I'm spending it with a beautiful girl. Those girls have tried everything to catch my attention. You did nothing but you caught my attention."

"What do you want from me?"

"I want nothing from you. Well maybe your name. That might be helpful." He placed his arm on the chair next to him and Ashley sighed again.

"Ashley Denorro."

The man smiled at her. "Dante Hastings."

"What?"

He chuckled. "Dante is my name."

And for the first time since they've met, she laughed. "Nice to meet you Dante."

A grin spread over his face. "Nice to meet you too, Ashley."

.

.

.

Ashley never in a million years thought that she was going to be doing this. She had always thought that everything would go exactly how she wanted it to go. But life had different thoughts and plans in mind for her.

Never in a million did she thought that she would be sitting with Dante and two of their lawyers, discussing their divorce.

"You guys never made a prenuptial agreement?" Thomas, Dante's lawyer asked them. He shuffled through his papers and glanced at Dante.

"We didn't really see the need to back then. Clearly, I was wrong." Dante said coldly, staring at Ashley. He intertwined his hands and placed them on the table.

Ashley held back her tears and just shook her head. "We-I thought that we didn't need to since I was so confident that we were going to be together."

Mayla, her best friend and lawyer, grabbed her hand and sent her a reassuring smile.

Ashley shot her a grateful one back.

"So how do you wish to divide up the shares?" Thomas glanced at Dante and then at Ashley. "Not to mention the custody for your child."

"Children." Ashley corrected him.

She looked at Dante. "I'm going to take full custody of them." She said softly, not taking her eyes off of him.

When she saw no emotion in his eyes, she felt her heart breaking even more. She had thought that it was impossible for her heart to break so much but clearly, this was only just the beginning.

"Is that okay Dante?" Mayla asked coldly.

"I want nothing to do with those bastard children." His words sent daggers into Ashley's heart and the emotionless expression on his face made her want to burst out into tears.

She stood up and glared at him through her tears. "How dare you call them bastards! What kind of a father are you?" she shouted out, feeling tears of anger rushing down her face.

"That's just it. I'm not a father." Dante replied coldly.

"How could you?" she whispered.

"Ashley." Mayla said softly, tugging her hand.

Ashley wiped away her tears and sat down again. She looked away from Dante, not wanting to see him see the pain behind her eyes. "They're yours and you know it Dante. The fact that you would call them that hurts me so much. You're their father." She said softly.

"They're not mine. You and I both know it." He said chuckling darkly. "She gets nothing Thomas. I want everything I own and everything I gave her during our marriage back. She doesn't deserve any of it."

"You insolent pig," Mayla said calmly, standing up abruptly. Fire burned in her eyes despite her attempts at remaining calm. "Ashley has been nothing but faithful to you. This is how you repay her?"

"Ms. Reilly, please calm down." Thomas said coolly. "Don't act so rash and unprofessional."

"I am calm." she hissed out. "I may be a lawyer but I'm a friend first, Mr. Quinton."

"Mayla, please." Ashley said softly. "Sit down."

Mayla scoffed and sat back down again. "Ashley deserves some if not all of his fortune. She started Hastings Enterprises. Without her funds, Hastings Enterprises would have never started."

"It was built on Dante's hand-work. She did nothing but give out money." Thomas said coldly, staring down at Mayla.

"Mr. Quinton, without her funds, Hastings Enterprises would never have the success that it has today. And it's all thanks to Ashley." Mayla said, glaring at Thomas.

"Ms. Reilly, must I remind you that-"

"Enough." Ashley said softly. She looked up from her lap and glanced at all three people in the room. "I want nothing from him. He can have everything back. It doesn't matter anymore."

"Ashley-" Mayla started.

Ashley interrupted her. "No. I want absolutely nothing."

"Very well." Mayla sighed. "Are we done here then?"

Everyone nodded their heads. Mayla looked at Ashley. "Ashley."

"I'm done." She whispered softly, standing up. Her hands instinctively, went to her neck where the necklace that Dante had gotten her for her birthday lay. It had been a few days before their wedding.

She froze as the memory of that day came to her mind.

.

.

.

"Close your eyes, mia bella." Dante whispered into her ear, standing behind her.

Ashley giggled and did what he said. She felt him moving her hair away from her neck and shivered when his fingers brushed through the sensitive part of her neck. C cold object touched her neck and she touched it.

"Open." He whispered.

She opened her eyes and looked down at the object. Her eyes started watering when she saw the beautiful necklace that resided on her neck. Turning around, she wrapped her arms around her fiancee's neck and hugged him tightly.

"Happy birthday, mia bella." He kissed the top of her head and she relished in his love.

"Dante, it's beautiful." She pulled away from him and touched the necklace, smiling.

He brushed a piece of her hair out of her face and smiled lovingly at her. "Not as beautiful as you, mia bella." He leaned down and captured her lips, sending her all of his love.

Ashley kissed back with the same amount of passion, wrapping her arms around his neck. Pulling away, she leaned her head against his and smiled. "I love you Dante."

"I love you, Ashley."

.

.

.

The tears brimmed her eyes again as she stared at the necklace.

Memories after memories of them crossed through her mind.

The time where they had their first date, their first kiss, their wedding day, the day of his success with his business. They all came rushing back to her and she could do nothing to stop it.

Her thoughts were consumed by him and by the memories that they shared.

Every part of her belonged to him. Her heart, her mind, her soul. It was all his to take. And he did take it but he gave it back to her, emptied.

He stole everything from her. Her feelings, her thoughts, her passion.

How could he just give everything away like this? Did he ever stop to think about how this is all affecting her? The supposed love of his life? Did he think twice before telling her about their divorce? Was this truly what he wanted?

She felt tears rolling again and she quickly took off the necklace. She could feel Dante's stare on her as she did it. She held it in her hands and stared down at it before looking up at him. She saw him looking down at the necklace before looking up at her.

She walked over to the other side of the table and grabbed his hand. "Here." She whispered.

She placed the necklace down on the palm on his hands and closed it up. "Here's the first thing you ever gave me." She said, trying to remain strong.

She smiled at him and took off her ring. She placed it on the table, never once taking her eyes off of him. "I hope this is what you really want." She whispered.

She hesitated for a second.

But then she reached up and kissed his cheek gently. "Goodbye Dante. I hope you have a nice life." She whispered.

She turned around and started walking out of the door where Mayla was waiting for her on the other side. She sent a small smile at Thomas.

He returned one half-heartedly.

She looked back at Mayla. "Let's go," she whispered.

Chapter 3

<hr>

C hapter 3

"Fancy seeing you here again today, Ashley." Dante said, taking a seat across from her. He sent a smile at her and waited for her to look up and see it.

It came to no surprise to him when he walked in and saw her sitting at the same table as the day before. Every time he came into the small café, there she was, sitting down, drinking coffee, all while reading the same book over and over again.

Her eyes slowly adverted from the book. Dante saw a small smiling gazing her lips as she took sight of him. "Aren't I always here?" she asked coyly before returning back to the damn book.

He frowned for a second due to the fact that Ashley didn't pay attention to him for more than ten seconds before turning back to the book. He then chuckled as he realized how unique she was and how her being more drawn by the book drew him in even more.

For the past four days, he had been coming into the café just to see her face. There was something about her that drew him in.

Maybe it was the vibe that she gave out.

Innocent and pure.

Or maybe it was the way she ignored the social norms of today and instead does her own little things.

Many girls failed to draw him in as Ashley had done. Those cleavages that they would flaunt his way did nothing to him now that he had met Ashley.

She got all of his attention and he didn't mind it at all. She wasn't like most girls and that's what he liked most about her.

She was her own person.

"Are you always reading?" he asked, taking a sip of his coffee that he had gotten from Starbucks earlier.

"I'm a book worm. What else can I say?" She replied, shrugging her shoulders. She placed her book down on the table gently and smiled at him. "So how was your day?"

Dante was stunned. "This was the first time that you have ever asked me that question. Mia bella, am I worming my way into your heart?" He teased, chuckling when he saw the famous scowl plastered on her pretty face.

How he loved seeing that cute little scowl.

"If this is the result of me being a nice person to you, then I'm never doing it again." Though her sentence might have some annoyed, there a hint of playfulness in her voice, letting him know that she was only joking.

Dante chuckled and leaned back against his seat, raising an eyebrow up at her.

"And since when are you ever nice to people? If I recall correctly, you were snapping at some random girl yesterday for absolutely nothing. Frankly, I'm a little surprised that you haven't given me any snide comments yet."

Another chuckle fell out of his lips when he saw her pouting, crossing her arms over her chest. It made her chest look even bigger than it already was and Dante held back a groan.

"I'm nice! And it wasn't just for nothing. She made me spill my coffee all over my new book!" She defended herself.

"All of that just for a book?" He shook his head at her and tsked. "You don't have any nice bones in your body huh?" he quirked an eyebrow up at her and smirked.

"I can be nice." she scoffed and uncrossed her arm. She pointed her index finger at him. "Just not to you."

"If you're such a nice person, give me a compliment." He leaned forward and pushed her finger away softly.

Sparks erupted where his fingers touched hers and he tried his best to ignore it.

"There's nothing nice to say about you." Amusement flashed through Ashley's eye and she smirked at him.

Dante gasped dramatically and placed his hand over his heart. "Mia bella, you wound me!"

Ashley rolled her eyes. "It's true though. I can't think of one nice thing to say to you." She teased.

Dante chuckled. "Mia bella, there's a whole lot of nice things that you can say about me. I bet there's one floating around in that pretty little head right now."

Ashley raised one of her eyebrows up. "Oh really? And what might that nice thought be? Amuse me Dante. I haven't had any good amusements in a few days."

"Well, you might be thinking about how hot or sexy I am." He smirked at her.

She shrugged her shoulders. "You're alright."

Dante glared at her. "What do you mean by alright?"

Ashley smirked again. "I've seen better."

Dante didn't know why but the comment that Ashley made just now caused him to see red everywhere.

She has seen better? Is this jealousy that's running through him right now?

"Oh really?" he said through gritted teeth.

Ashley deepened her smirk. "Really."

"Well I guess I'm just going to have to change that." He smirked.

"Good luck with that."

.

.

.

Dante looked down at the necklace in his hands. The necklace that Ashley had given back to him. It felt cold to the touch and he put it on the table.

The room felt like it was shaking underneath his feet and he sat down on the chair. Everything was spinning around and changing. He didn't know how to stop it.

He loosened up his tie and sighed.

He looked at the necklace again and grabbed it. Walking out of the room, he ran down the stairs as fast as he could. When he reached the receptionist's desk, he quickly threw the question at her. "Did Ashley and Mayla leave yet?"

"Yes sir. They turned right about twenty seconds ago." She said, biting down on her bottom lip. "You might want to hurry if you want to catch up to them."

"Thank you..." he trailed off.

"Jasmine Sir." She said with a soft smile.

He nodded his head and thanked her again. He ran out the door and turned to the right. He saw Ashley standing by herself and walked up to her. He grabbed her hand roughly and placed the necklace in her palm, giving her a glare.

"I gave you this before we got married. I don't want it. You keep it." He said coldly, trying his best to keep his voice cold and distant.

Her eyes looked down at the necklace and he saw a tear slipping out of her eyes. "Don't cry." He huffed. "Nothing you do can make me change my mind." He turned his head towards the other side of the street, not wanting to look at her face.

He heard a scoff coming out from her. Curious as to why he made that sound, he turned to her and gave her a calculating look. "What?"

A dry laugh came out of her lips. "You think I'm crying to get you to be mine again?" she shook her head and he saw tears continuing to fall down her face.

Yet her voice remained strong. "I'm crying because I don't want any reminders of you anymore. These babies are enough for me Dante. I gave this necklace back to you for a reason."

"They're not mine. They shouldn't remind you of me." He hissed out, shoving his hands inside his pant pockets. "Stop making it seem like they are."

"You know what? Go to hell." She shouted. She threw the necklace on the ground and turned her body. "I never ever want to see you again."

"That's something that we could agree on. I don't know why I was even interested in you in the first place. You were a b*tch back then and you're one now. That's probably why your dad didn't hesitate to ship you off." He blurted out, instantly regretting what he said.

He saw her whole body stiffening. The soft sobs that came out of her caused his heart to break into a million of pieces. No matter what she did. No matter how many times she wronged him, he still loves her.

There was no one else that he can love as much as he loved her.

"I hate you." She whispered.

She then turned around and gave him her most hated look. "Once you realize your mistake, it would be too late Dante. Have a good life." She shouted before running away from him.

"I want to hate you, but I can't." he whispered. "You were the only woman I have ever loved and the only woman that I will love. You're my first and my last." He whispered.

He knelt down and pick up the necklace. "I love you Ashley." He whispered, pocketing the necklace into his pants. He started walking back to office.

Each step he took caused his heart to break even further. He felt his eyes becoming glossy and held back his tears as best as he could.

When he was in the building again, he walked towards the elevator and clicked the button for Thomas's office.

Although the ride only lasted ten seconds, to him it felt more like ten years. When it opened, he walked into Thomas's office and sat down on the couch.

"You okay man?" He heard Thomas whispering.

Looking up, he saw Thomas giving him a worried look. In his hands held the folder that was to be sent to the city office tomorrow morning. The folder that would soon cut off all ties with him and Ashley. He glared at it and closed his eyes.

"No, I can't ever be okay now, Thomas. My life is nothing without Ashley." He said dejectedly. He put his arm over his head and sighed deeply. "I don't know how I'm supposed to continue life without her. I can't be the same without her."

"Why did you divorce her then? Why cause not only one heart to break but two?" Thomas's voice held disappointment and a little bit of scorn.

Dante knew that Thomas didn't fully support the divorce. He had tried on countless occasion to convince Dante to reconsider but it never worked. Thomas firmly believed that Dante was wrong but that was only because he didn't fully know the reason why.

Dante was about to reply to him when his phone rang. He removed his arm and took his phone out of his pocket. Looking down and his face furrowed in confusion when he saw that it was an unknown number.

"Who is it?" Thomas asked. Dante felt him standing behind him, staring down at the phone also. "Dante who's that?"

Dante rolled his eyes at him. "How am I suppose to know? It says unknown."

"Well pick it up and see who it is." Thomas retorted.

Dante slid his finger across his phone and put it on speaker. "Hello? Who's this?"

Nothing.

There was nothing on the other end.

"Hello? Who's this?" Dante repeated with more force.

There was a quick laugh before the call ended. Dante looked at the phone and looked at Thomas.

A bing gained his attention and he looked down again. His face paled when he saw what it was and he felt his heart beating faster in his chest.

"Dante what is it?"

Dante shook his head and gulped. "You want to know the reason why I divorced Ashley? Why I think those babies aren't mine?" He turned to look at Thomas.

Thomas furrowed his eyebrow. "Why?"

Dante showed Thomas his phone and watched as Thomas's face contorted to one of confusion. "Is that?"

"Ashley." Dante spat the name as if it was poison.

"I can't believe this."

It was a picture of Ashley, in today's clothing, standing outside of a café. One hand held the same folder that she had today while the other was wrapped around another man's neck. She was standing on her tippy-toes and her lips were touching those of the man.

A man that was not Dante.

The man wore a red coat and sunglasses, shielding his face and frame from recognition.

"Wait there's a message." Thomas muttered.

Dante took back his phone and looked down. His beating stopped when he saw what the message said.

I won.

.

.

.

Who do you guys think the mysterious sender is? ;)

So I know this was supposed to be up yesterday but I forgot! I'm so sorry! I deeply apologize! I'll try to update this friday to make up for lost time!

The banner to the side was made by @SudeshnaDey12. Thank you so much for the beautiful banner! It's beautiful. This chapter is also dedicated to you girl!

Send me covers/banners at Ambyluvsz@Gmail.com.

Next update is: May 15th or before!

Love you all of my lovely owlers!

~Amber <3 <3 <3

~Amber <3 <3 <3

Chapter 4

- -

C hapter 4

"Why hello there Ashley. Where are you off to?"

Ashley turned her head around and groaned when she saw him. She hugged her books tighter to her chest and glared at him as he stood next to her, too close for comfort.

Using her index finger, she pushed his chest away, ignoring how his rock hard chest made her feel a little dizzy. "Ever heard of personal space mister?"

"With you mia bella? Nope." he replied with a toothy grin, popping the 'p'. He leaned his body against the wall and smirked at her. "Where are you off to?"

"Class." she rolled her eyes and continued walking again. She felt him walking besides her and fought to keep the smile off her face.

"Class? What's that?" he said with mock confusion.

"It's a place where those with goals and ambitions go in order to be success-ful." She turned to him and smirked. "Two things that you clearly lack."

"Ouch. Is it going to be like this every single time?"

"What? Me pointing out how incapable you are of learning?" Ashley stopped and turned to him, giving him a sickly sweet smile. "Seems like it."

"You wound me. My ego dropped down three sizes since meeting you." he placed his hand over his heart and sighed dramatically. "My heart can't take anymore mia bella. Please say something nice to help me feel better."

"I don't feel like feeding your ego. Any larger and people won't be able to see your," she glanced down before looking up and smirking at him, "little friend."

"I'll have you know, there's nothing little about me." he said in a deadpan voice.

"That's what they all say." Ashley replied.

"That hurts. Say something nice and maybe I'll forgive you." Dante grinned.

"I never asked for your forgiveness." Ashley replied.

"But you need it." Dante shoved her shoulder gently. "Come on Ash. Just one little comment."

Ashley just gave him a blank look. She poked his chest, "Nothing nice to say about you." her eyes danced with amusement when he gave her his unimpressed look.

"There's a lot mia bella."

"I don't recall any."

"Did we not have this conversation before?" he placed his finger under his chin as if thinking. "Ah yes we did. Yesterday to be exact."

"And we will only have to same conversation everyday so might as well stop bothering me." Ashley didn't know why but her heart tugged painfully when she had said that.

She didn't know why but the thought of not being able to see Dante made her sad beyond compare.

"On one condition."

She felt her heart stop. Did this mean that he would actually leave her alone?

She gulped and faked a smile at him. "Joy what do I have to do to get rid of you."

"Go on a date with me."

Ashley gaped. She dropped her books to the ground at just stared at him, not believing what had just came out of his mouth. "W-what?"

Dante nodded his head. Bending down, he picked up her books and held them in his right hand. His left hand went behind his neck and scratched it nervously. "Yeah. Go on a date with me and if you don't enjoy it then I'll never bother you again."

Ashley stared at him with her mouth wide open. She closed it and looked around. Her eyes moved back and forth.

"So what do you say?" Dante smiled hopefully.

Ashley smiled at him and nodded her head. "Alright. I'll go on a date with you. Just so I can finally get rid of your ugly fat face." she smirked and took her books out of his hands and started walking away.

"Why do you always ruin our moments?!" Dante shouted after her with strong amusement lacing his voice.

Ashley chuckled to herself and turned back. She sent him a small smile that he returned before walking into her class.

.

.

.

Ashley and Mayla sat down at the coffee table. Things were silent. Not a single word was exchanged between the two.

Ashley looked down at her belly and her eyes teared up again like it has been doing for the past few weeks. She placed her hand on her stomach and looked away, trying to blink back the tears.

Her hand slowly caressed her stomach and she snapped her eyes shut, wanting to block the whole world out.

It was only her and her babies now.

No one else but them.

Everyone seems to abandon her at one point but her babies will never know what it feels like to be abandoned.

She will make sure that they have all the love that they need to prosper in this world. She will make sure that they will never know what it feels like to be left behind, to be hurt by those who were suppose to love them unconditionally.

"Ashley,"

Ashley opened her eyes and looked at Mayla, her eyes doing all the talking that she needed. She couldn't dare risk talking right now. It would only make her feel worse than she already did. And right now, she didn't to remain as calm as possible.

Mayla sighed and glanced away. Her finger traced the rim of the coffee cup that seemed to just had appeared out of nowhere. Mayla had probably ordered it while she was lost in her thoughts.

Ashley glanced down and noticed a cup of water also sitting in front of her. She smiled gratefully at Mayla when Mayla had looked into her eyes.

"I know this may sound bad but maybe it's time for you to return to Italy." Mayla muttered.

Ashley gulped. She picked up her cup and gripped it. "Why?"

Mayla turned away and looked at the people that were passing through. "Think about it Ashley. Italy is the last place anyone would go to look for you."

Ashley closed her eyes and leaned back against the chair. She felt her whole world falling apart right in front of her but could do nothing to help it stay the way it was. It only seemed to fall even harder every time she tried to fix it up.

"I think that's a good idea." she opened her eyes and brought the cup to her lips. Her tears fell down slowly and she smiled sadly at Mayla. "But with what money Mayla? I'm practically broke. I have nothing left but the clothes that I'm wearing."

Mayla smiled at her and shook her head. "You're my best friend. You don't need to worry about a thing. I'll have everything covered for you."

Ashley laughed humorlessly. "Worry is the only thing I can do right now." She looked away. "God I feel so useless."

Mayla slapped her shoulders gently. "Don't you dare say that ever again."

"Mayla,"

"No. You're the strongest girl I know. You've been through so much yet you're still here. You're still trying to continue on living, knowing how hard everything will be." Tears brimmed Mayla's eyes.

Ashley smiled at Mayla's words and placed her hand on top of hers. "Thank you Mayla." she whispered. "But I still don't know how I'm suppose to survive in Italy with two newborns. It's not possible."

Her heart broke with the thought of not being able to provide for her children's needs. "My children are going to hate me for not giving them everything they deserve."

Mayla scowled and slapped Ashley's cheek softly enough so that it doesn't hurt her but hard enough for her to stop being so insecure about herself.

"Enough Ashley. You are forgetting who your best friend is. I can get you a place in Italy with no problem at all. Trust me." her eyes softened. "I would never let you down like your asshole of a father or your bastard of a husband."

Ashley laughed lightly and smiled gratefully at Mayla. "Thank you Mayla. I know I can always count on you."

Mayla nodded her head and grinned. "Of course. I'd do anything for you, Ash. You should know that by now. You're like the little sister I never had."

"Thank you for always taking care of me." Ashley whispered. Her eyes teared up again but instead of it being tears of sadness, this time, it was tears filled with joy and gratefulness. "I don't know where I'll be without you."

Mayla placed her other hand on top of Ashley's. "No I have to thank you. Thank you for giving me strength in my darkest times Ash. You have done so much for me and this is only one step in me repaying all you have ever done for me."

"Best friends for life." Ashley muttered.

Mayla nodded her head in agreement. "Best friends for life."

.

.

.

Mayla grabbed her stuff from the table. She looked down at Ashley and placed a hand on her shoulder. "Everything will be okay. I need to get back to the firm. Call me if you need anything."

Ashley nodded her head. She stood up and hugged Mayla. "Thank you for everything you have done for me."

Mayla smiled and nodded her head. "I'll see you soon."

Ashley took her stuff off the table and started walking down the streets of Sunset Blvd. Her put her hands into her pockets and glanced aimlessly in front of her, not knowing where to go.

A flash of red fabric met her eyes become she bumped into someone.

Files fell down to the ground.

Ashley cursed and she reached down, beginning to pick up the papers. "I'm sorry, I wasn't looking at where I was going."

Her head looked up and she gulped. She stood up and handed the files to him.

Although she hasn't seen him ever since they were kids, she could recognize him everywhere. "Rafael," she muttered.

Rafael grabbed his papers and looked at her from head to toe. A smile came to his lips. "Bella," he breathed out, "I haven't seen you in some time."

Ashley nodded her head. "I-I have to go," she whispered.

She turned around to walk away but he grabbed her hand and turned her back.

"Ashley," he said. "Why did you leave?"

She smiled weakly at him. "Italy was not meant for me at the time."

Rafael released her hand. His hands moved up and touched her cheek. "What about now?"

Ashley took a step back, dropping her smile. "I have to go."

Rafael grinned at her and nodded. "I'll see you soon, Ashley. Until then."

Ashley nodded her head and walked away from him. She reached deeper into her pocket and pulled out her phone.

Her fingers typed in a number that she hasn't used in over fifteen years. Her fingers hesitated to click the call button. She sighed and sat down at a cafe and pressed it, praying that the number never changed.

She knew she could regret her decision but she couldn't let Mayla pay for everything.

Mayla had done enough for her already.

It's time for her to step up and take control of her life. Even if it means going back to the one she ran away from.

"Hello." A gruff voice answered.

"Hello papa." she muttered into the phone.

"Ashley?" she heard a slight shuffle before he came back again, this time his voice louder than before. "Is that you?"

"Yes papa." she felt tears welled into her eyes again at the memory of the last time she saw him.

When she had asked to go live with her grandparents and he had told her that it was the best idea she had in her whole entire life. He proceeded to tell her about how she had disappointed him as a daughter.

"Ashley, I haven't heard from you in fifteen years. I'm sorry Ashley for the way I have treated you." he whispered. His voice sounded broken and aged.

"It's okay papa. I forgive you." she whispered. "Papa."

"Yes mia figlia?"

"I'm coming home." She smiled and closed her eyes. "I'm coming home papa."

"I will see you when you get here then." he muttered. "Until then." he hung up the phone.

Ashley stood up and placed her phone back into her pockets. She smiled and walked off, already leaving her old life behind her. She's never coming back here. Not even if her life depended on it.

.

.

.

Hi guys. So I just wanted to get this chapter out as fast as I could to make up for lost time. But let's face it. No matter how fast I put it out, it's still not enough to make it up to you guys. :((But I promise you that this will never happen again. I won't leave until all the books I have started are finish and that's a promise that I will force myself to keep.

So I haven't really written this book in a while and my inspiration for it is really rough and choppy. I will go back and edit it once my mind is back with this book again. ((:

Despite that, I still hope you guys enjoy and yeah. ((:

Love you all of my lovely owlers!

~Amber <3 <3 <3 (Man I haven't said that in forever)

Chapter 5

Okay first thing I need to point out is that I'm sorry for those who I have disappointed by rewriting this whole entire book. I got a message today asking me to put up the old version again and it's not the first time someone has asked me either. Trust me. I got a lot of messages like that. But I can't for two reason. One reason being that the file I had containing all the chapters from the old version got corrupted and I can't get it back. The second being that Delilah (foreverinfinities) and I are two different kind of writers. The way she envisioned the book wasn't the way I envisioned it. And we both agreed that in order for me to write this book as best as I could, I had to change it up and make it match my style of writing. It might be worse than before, it might be better than before. But at least this time, it's written through my style, making it easier for me. So I'm sorry but I can't change it or put it back up again. Yes Delilah did work really hard on this but I just can't. Now there will be points of the book where it will seem similar but not really. So many got confused on the characters and couldn't even remember who was who. This version will help you hopefully remember them better.

With that being said, Enjoy. ((:

Chapter 5

Ashley smoothed out the wrinkles on her dress and looked into the mirror. She smiled and tucked a piece of hair behind her ear, satisfied with what she was seeing. She took her lip balm from the table and applied it onto her lips, smacking them together in the end.

"Ashley.Your boy toy is here." Mayla's voice shouted from the living room.

Ashley rolled her eyes at what Mayla was referring to Dante as and grabbed her clutch off the table. "He's not my boy toy." she muttered angrily as she passed by Mayla.

Mayla smiled at her innocently.

She glared at Mayla when she felt a slap on her left butt. "What was that for?"

Mayla winked at her and threw herself on the couch. "For a little bit of luck in case you get lucky." She winked at Ashley and did some perverted motions with her fingers and tongue.

"Are you guys forgetting that I'm standing right here?"

Ashley turned around and blushed when she saw Dante standing there with an amused smirk on his face. She turned around and glared at Mayla who only looked at her innocently.

She turned back around and smiled at Dante. "Hi." she said softly.

"Hi." he grinned and her and held up a bouquet of flowers. "These are for you. I hope you like lilies."

I love lilies, she thought to herself.

She grabbed the bouquet and smiled thankfully at him. "Thank you. I love lilies. Let me find a vase to put these in and we'll go." Her whole body turned only to have her head bumped into another. "Ouch. What the heck Mayla?" she rubbed her forehead.

Mayla used one hand to rub her forehead while the other snatched the bouquet out of Ashley's hands.

She smirked. "I'll put them in for you. You go and enjoy your little date." She pushed Ashley aside and glared at Dante. "Hurt her in any shape way or form, and I swear, you will regret the day you met me."

Dante only responded to her response with a raised eyebrow. He looked passed her and smiled at Ashley. "You ready now?" He saw Mayla coming closer to possibly hurt him but he only put his arm out and pushed her head out of the way.

Ashley nodded her head and walked towards him. "Behave." she hissed lowly to Mayla while giving Dante a tight smile.

"I already don't like him." Mayla muttered back.

Ashley took Dante's outstretched hand. "Where are we going?" she asked him as Mayla closed the door behind her.

Dante grinned down at her.

Ashley felt her heart beating just a little faster. Her body began to heat up with the familiar blush coming to her face. She looked away from him. She didn't know what he was doing to her but she knew that she didn't like it one bit.

"It's a surprise." he winked at her.

.

.

.

Dante grinned at Ashley and grabbed her hand, pulling her towards the middle of the forest. "Come on." he urged her when he saw her looking around nervously.

"You didn't take me here to kill me did you?" Ashley looked up at him with nervous eyes and pouty lips. Lips that Dante wished he could kiss.

Dante shook his head, released her hand, and broke into a short jog. "If I did, you would already be dead."

He laughed when he turned around and saw her trying to keep up with him. He took her arm again and started pulling her along with him.

Ashley scowled at him and tried to move faster to keep up with him while trying her best not to trip and fall.

She knew that if she did, there would be a chance of her falling on top of Dante or even under him. She knew for a fact that Dante wouldn't mind that happening at all but she knew enough about his reputation to make her fear for her heart.

Dante was a well known player and Ashley wasn't in the mood to get played.

Ever.

"Come on Ashley. Can you run any slower?" he teased her, dragging her faster. He laughed out loud when she stumbled a bit, almost falling over but she caught herself just in time.

Ashley stopped and glared at him, crossing her arms over her chest. She raised her eyebrow up at him. "Can you run any slower?"

Dante grinned at her. "Nope. Not possible."

"Then no I won't run any faster." And being the mature person that she was, she stuck her tongue out at him.

He smirked. "Well then I guess I have no choice."

Ashley gave him a confused look "No choice but to—hey! What are you doing? Put me down!" she shouted, smacking Dante's chest as he ran while carrying her bridal style.

Dante laughed and started to run even faster towards his destination. "You gave me no choice, mia bella!" he shouted through the wind.

"Dante! I'm wearing a freaking dress." she shouted while holding onto to her dress at her knee, making sure that it didn't fly up.

"All the more reasons to sweep you off your feet!" Dante grinned and then placed her down on the ground, standing in front of her so he blocks her view. "Cover your eyes." He said softly.

"Why?" she whined, moving her face around him but it was to no avail as he blocked her.

Damn he was like a giant.

Dante smirked and shrugged his shoulders. He then smiled a true and genuine smile. "Just do as I say."

Ashley sighed and closed her eyes. She then felt Dante's hands covering her eyes and groaned. "I'm not going to peek."

"I'm not going to take any chances." Was Dante's reply. "Okay now, I'm going to guide you. Listen okay."

"Listen? Listen to wha—"

"Sh. Just listen."

Ashley rolled her eyes inwardly and let Dante guide her to the place that he was so dying for her to see as their first date. She held onto his arms as they covered her eyes and groaned when she felt her foot accidentally hitting a tree. "Dante, I'm going to fall."

"Don't worry bella. I'll catch you." She could hear the smile in his voice and because of that, her own smile made its way to her lips.

"You better." She said with a smile.

"Of course. Now be quiet and just listen."

Ashley perked her ears up but frowned when she heard nothing. "What am I supposed to be listening to?"

"Sh."

She then heard it. It was soft but it was still there. It was like the sound of water hitting the pavement like rain but it was stronger than that. "Dante? Are we at a waterfall?"

Ashley felt her eyes being freed and her eyes widened when she saw the sight in front of her. "Ding ding ding. We have a winner." Dante whispered into her ear making her shiver.

Ashley looked at the waterfall in awe and closer towards it.

It wasn't big like most waterfalls, in fact, it was only about ten feet wide and twelve feet high. But nonetheless, it was still beautiful. The flowers surrounding it gave off the nature glow while the birds chirped happily on the trees.

"It's so beautiful." She whispered in awe.

"Yes. Yes she is."

Ashley turned to look at Dante. It wasn't surprising when she saw him staring at her. A teasing smile made its way to her lips. "Smooth."

Dante laughed and sat down on the ground. He winked at her. "I know."

Ashley laughed and sat down next to him. "So, this is your ideal of a first date?" she asked, turning to look at him.

He shook his head and smiled at her. "Depends on how special the girl is. If she's not then a movie would suffice but if she is then I would show her the beauties in everything and make sure that our date is special. Nothing like anyone have ever seen before."

Ashley smiled at him and looked towards the waterfall again. "So, what category do I fall under?" she asked in a joking manner but all in all, she was curious.

It was silence for a while and Ashley turned to Dante, seeing him looking at her with a smile on his face.

"You're special." He turned away from her. "You probably already know my reputation."

"You mean the sleeping around with random girls reputation?" though she meant in a joking way, a hint of bitterness seeped through.

Dante nodded his head. "None of those girls were special enough." He turned back to her. "But with you, you captivated me the second I saw you. I didn't just want to get you into my bed, I wanted to get to know you."

Ashley grinned inwardly to herself. "Oh."

Dante chuckled and continued. "With you, sex never came into my mind once. It was just you with your cute scowls, sarcastic remarks, and breathtaking smile. I found myself wanting to know more about you." he gave her a smile and kissed her cheek softly.

Ashley smiled at him. "I guess, I also want to know more about you also."

Dante grinned. "Well, I guess we're just going to have to bear with each other for the time."

Ashley laughed and leaned against him. "I guess so."

.

.

.

Ashley felt the driver pulling into the driveway of her childhood home. She looked out the window and felt the familiar feeling of being rejected building up in her veins.

The house looked the same as it did fifteen years ago. The same color though this time more vibrant due to it probably getting repainted. The yard was as green as ever and the familiar cars still parked in the middle of nowhere.

"We're here Ma'am." The cab driver informed her with a gentle smile.

Ashley reached into her pocket and pulled out some euros and handed it to him. She smiled warmly at him and opened the door. "Keep the change. Thank you for the ride."

The driver tipped his hat at her. "Thank you ma'am. Have a nice day."

"Thank you. You too." She grabbed her stuff from the seat next to her and got out of the cab fully. She pulled the handle of the luggage up and started walking towards the front door. Her heart pounded heavier with every single step that she took.

Knocking on the door, she held her breath as she waited for someone to open it.

Her eyes glanced around and she felt tears coming to her eyes when she saw the plate that she had made for her father hanging from a tree. She walked up to it and touched it gently. A small laugh came out of her mouth and she smiled.

He had kept this throughout all of these years?

For the past fifteen years, Ashley had thought her father hated her but through this, she's starting to believe that maybe she was wrong. Maybe he didn't hate her at all. Just disappointed that she wasn't the type of daughter that he had wanted.

But through this, he has proved that he still loves her.

The door finally opened and Ashley wiped her tears away quickly. She turned around and smiled when she saw him.

Her father.

"Hi Papa." she whispered softly. Her eyes welled up with tears again and she smiled at him. "I missed you."

Ashley didn't miss the way that her father's eyes light up when he saw her. She saw tears of happiness forming around his eyes and she ran into his arms and hugged him tightly.

The familiar smell of cinnamon and wood was still on his skin and she never remembered ever being so happy to smell it.

"Papa." she whispered. "I'm home."

"Mia figlia. I have missed you so much." he whispered into her ears, kissing the top of her head. "I have missed you so much."

Ashley let her tears fall and she continued staying in the embrace of her father. She knew that at this moment, things will only start looking up. Before her father had remarried, he was loving and very supportive towards her.

In her heart, Ashley knew, that that father never left.

.

.

.

Choppy but hopefully I'll get back into the mojo again ((:

Love you all of my lovely owlers.

~Amber, the mother of all owlers wonderfuls. <3 <3 <3

Chapter 6

Hello there beautiful people. ((: I literally spent three hours on this thing. Ugh. My mojo. Please come back to me soon.

Anyways, if some parts of it seem familiar then it should. ((: I was able to get back two chapters because apparently they were actually saved on wattpad. But the other chapters are gone sooo whoops? haha...

Hm...what else? Oh yes. I might only be able to update on weekends from now on. I'm now a very very busy girl. Junior year along with a crying newborn baby brother is never a good match. Especially when said brother is an attention seeking baby and won't settle for anything less. The little monster cries when no one pays attention to him. Is this all babies or is he just a special one?

Shout-outs to LorettaFox and IAmACaticorn. You guys are amazing and I'm so glad to call you guys my friends. <3 THANK YOU FOR DEFENDING ME! I APPRECIATE IT!

Okay guys! Enjoy! <3

.

.

Chapter 6

"Papa! Papa!" Ashley ran into her father's office with tears streaming down her face.

Her father turned around and faced her with a tired expression. "Ashley?"

She climbed onto his lap. She wrapped her arms around her father's neck and started to cry even harder.

Her father sighed in exasperation. "What is it now, Ashley?" he pushed her shoulders back a little and stared into her eyes. His face held only annoyance as he stared down at her, not that she even realized it.

"Samuel made me fall." she hiccuped and wiped her tears using the back of her hand. Sniffing, she climbed off his lap and sat down on the floor, staring up at him like she usually did even since she was a small child. "Papa make him stop."

"Ashley I don't have time for this. Samuel would never do such a thing. Now go to your room. I'm busy." He gave her a hard stare before turning around to face his work.

Ashley stood up from the ground and glared at her father's back. Her tears fell down but this time, it was because of how her father has been treating her lately. Ever since he married the 'love' of his life. "Papa, you don't understand. Samuel is mean."

"Ashley, I will not tolerate this anymore! Grow up!" her father yelled at her. His face locked with hers and he glared at her harshly. "You will learn to get along with Samuel. He is always so kind to you. Stop being a brat."

Ashley was shocked. Her father has never yelled at her before let alone call her a brat. Every time, he would always sternly tell her something but would never raise his voice up at her.

She has never seen this side of her father before and it scared her immensely.

She knew that her father could see the fear written on her face but he did nothing to make it go away. If anything, he only made it worse by glaring at her so harshly.

She stepped back. Her eyes was wide and filled with fear but her father's remained angry and not the least bit regretful.

He has changed.

She turned around quickly and ran off to her room. Her eyes were spilling with tears and when she got there, she threw herself onto her bed and cried. Her whole body shook with tears and there was nothing that she could do to stop it.

Just like there was nothing for her to do to stop her life from spinning so out of control.

.

.

.

There were only clanks and the sound of food being chewed at dinner that night. The room was tense and everyone knew it.

Especially Ashley.

She twirled her fork around her spaghetti while her head was rested on her palm. Her eyes were still red and swollen from the crying session that she did earlier while her body continued to shake every once in awhile.

"Ashley." her father's voice echoed through the room.

Ashley stopped and placed her fork on the plate. She glanced up slowly and stared passed her father's head. "Yes papa?" her voice was soft but hoarse.

He gave her a stare down. "Do you have anything you wish to say to Samuel?"

Her head turned to Samuel's and hatred build in her when she saw the mischievous gleam in his eyes. His face was filled with fake hurt.

No one seemed to see past his facade besides Ashley and his mother.

Alessandra sent him a quick smirk. She turned to Ashley and winked at her before looking down at her food again.

Ashley silently wished for her to choke.

Ashley clenched her fists under the table and smiled fakely at Samuel. "Samuel, I apologize for my actions this morning." she recited the words that her father has forced her to repeat.

"It's okay Ashley." Samuel said with a smile.

"Now was that so hard?" Her father spoke up.

Ashley glared at him. She stood up and pushed her chair back. "I want to go live with nonno and nonna."

Her father's fork dropped onto the plate, making a loud 'clank'. "What did you just say?"

Ashley looked down timidly and played with the hem of her dress. "Nonno wants me to go live with him and nonna." She looked up again, feeling confidence spiked in her, and stared straight into her father's eyes. "Unlike you, they care for me!"

Her father looked taken back and only stared at her. After a while, he picked up his fork and continued eating again. "Very well. You may go. No ungrateful daughter of mine is going to live in my house."

"Fine!" Ashley shouted. She pushed her chair down and ran up to her room. Only one thought ran in her brain.

I hate him.

.

.

.

"Your room is still the same. I just put in a bigger bed. " Antonio smiled at Ashley and turned towards the stairs. "You can figure out what to change and I'll send some people to change it however you like."

Ashley nodded her head. "Thank you papa." she muttered quietly.

He gave her a tight smile in return. There was a part of him that knows that things can never go back to the way they use to and Ashley cannot trust in him the way that she used to.

He still hoped that things will return back to normal. That she would look at him like she used too.

Like he was her hero.

"Of course Ashley. I'd do anything for you. You're my daughter." he kissed her forehead. He had noticed her wincing when he did that and stepped away slowly. He hid his hurt behind his usual mask. "Why don't you get settled in and meet me in the kitchen?"

Her only response was a nod. She rolled her suitcase to the stairs but stopped when she realized the problem. Her room was on the third floor and there was no way that she could carry this suitcase.

It would put too much pressure on her and the babies.

"Wait papa." she called to him.

Antonio turned around and looked at her. "Yes mia figlia?"

A blush appeared on her face and she looked at him nervously. "Can you help me with my suitcase. I- uh- I can't carry anything heavy."

Antonia looked at her in confusion. He walked over to her and picked up her suitcase. "If you don't mind me asking, why can't you?" He asked her as they walked up the stairs.

He noticed that her eyes would close sometimes and her face would fill up with pain once in awhile.

"I'm pregnant." she said softly.

Antonio stopped and stared at her.

She turned away from his glance and stared at the wall. Her eyes came face to face with a baby picture of her and she smiled gently at it. Her eyes diverted to her stomach and she hopes that her babies would come out looking healthy and as beautiful as ever.

"How long?" he choked out.

"Four months papa." she muttered. She continued walking again, not glancing back to see if he was following her or not. "My husband and I are divorced."

"You were married?"

"Yes Papa. For a few years actually." She muttered. "I don't like talking about it."

And I can't trust you yet to tell you. She thought to herself.

.

.

.

Dante groaned and buried his head into his hands. The memories of his ex-wife played over and over in his mind like a broken record. He couldn't stop it no matter how hard he tried. He so badly wanted to forget about her but she had already claimed the spot in his brain.

Why can't he forget about her? Why is it so hard to just let her go? She wasn't the woman he thought she was. She was evil, conniving, unfaithful, but yet, he still loves her.

Dante heard his door opening and he looked up to see his mother coming in with a solemn look on her face. "Mother." He stood up and walked over to her, kissing her cheek. His mother smiled at him weakly and sat down.

"Dante. We need to talk." She said softly.

"About?" he sat down next to her and turned his body to face her.

"Ashley." She whispered.

Dante froze when he heard her name. A scowl then took over his face. "Mother, I thought we agreed to never mention that woman ever again."

"She left the country, Dante." His mother said. She sighed. "Mayla had called me this morning to tell me that by the time you realize your mistake, Ashley won't be here any longer."

Dante felt his heart constricting with pain. He snapped his eyes shut and leaned back against his seat. Memories of her continued playing and he felt a traitorous tear escape his eyes. "It's for the best, mother." He croaked out.

"But Dante, what about the babies?" there was worry in his mother's voice and Dante knew it would break her heart when he tells her the truth.

"They're not mine." He whispered.

"What? What are you talking about?"

Dante opened his eyes and smiled grimly at his mother who looked at him with shock in her eyes. "They're not mine, mother."

"Dante, of course they're yours." His mother said with tears in her eyes.

"They're not. She cheated on me mother. That's why I divorced her." he buried his head into his hands again. "She cheated."

.

.

.

Hope you guys enjoyed that!

Have a beautiful day/night wherever you are and remember the greater your storm, the brighter your rainbow!

Love you all of my lovely owlers!

~Amber <3 <3 <3

Chapter 7

I am so sorry! This is like almost a month late! Sorry guys! I've been super busy lately because I always end up knocking out so early so my homework has been piling up and imma stop now. I don't think you guys want to read me ramble on and on. HAHA! So...Update Saturday hopefully. I'm praying that my teachers see mercy and not give me so much homework this weekend. I pray!

Anyways, enjoy. <3 <3 <3

.

.

.

Chapter 7

There was a small deafening silence before it happened. The soft cries of a newborn baby lit up the room and caused everyone to sigh in relief. It was loud but soft, with the promise of a good future for the couple.

Antonio leaned his forehead against his wife and kissed her cheek.

"You did well, my dear." he whispered lovingly into her ear. He took her hand and brushed his wife's hair back and smiled. "She's finally here."

A sigh of relief and happiness left his wife's mouth. She tried to sit up and laid down again, pain clear in her eyes.

"Antonio I want to see her." she whispered. She squeezed his hand and smiled up at him. "I want to see our baby. Our dear little Ashley."

"Here she is." The doctor handed a cleaned Ashley to Antonio and smiled down. "She's perfectly healthy. Ten fingers and ten toes."

Antonio took the baby into his arms carefully, cradling her head on the side of his elbow. Her small body fit so perfectly in his arms and he smiled down at her. Tears of happiness flooded into his eyes and his heart opened even wider. "Hello there little Ashley. I'm your papi."

The small girl looked up at him and gurgled. Her hands reached up slowly and she touched his chin. A hint of a smile came onto her lips. Her eyes closed and she fell into a slumber. Her chest moved up and down and she rested comfortably on her father's arm.

"Isabella look at her my dear. She's resting so well." Antonio looked down at his wife. His smiled instantly left his face when he saw her, eyes opened but chest not moving. "Isabella? Darling?" He whispered.

She didn't move. Her eyes were empty and lifeless while her body remained still and pale.

As if sensing something wrong, Ashley instantly woke up and began crying.

"Doctor!" Antonio shouted. He held his daughter closer to his body, shielding her eyes to protect her.

Though she would have no memory of this, Antonio already felt as if he had to protect Ashley from all horrible images that might taint her mind.

"Nurses get Dr. Serins." Dr. Carson turned to Antonio and gave him a stern look. "Antonio you have to get out of here now."

"No! I have to stay here! She's my wife!" Antonio shouted. His ears failed to hear the soft cries of his daughter, yearning for the touch of her mother.

"Antonio, please!" The doctor shouted. He gave Antonio a sympathetic look. "Give Ashleh to one of the nurses and leave. We can't save her if you're here. I promise we'll try our best."

Antonio faintly remember the nurse taking Ashley away. The next thing he remembers is standing outside of the emergency room, waiting for the doctor to come out and give him the news that he knew was true.

He had seen her. He had seen her pale and lifeless face. He had seen her whole body slumped against the bed with no movement in her chest. He knew that he had lost her. He knew that she had left him, had left their child motherless.

Antonio's body slumped against the wall. He pulled his knees to his chest and buried his head in it. The fingers on his hands tugged on his hair tightly but he did not feel the pain.

The only pain he felt was the one in his heart, knowing that the only woman he has ever loved is now gone forever.

He didn't know what to do now. Before Isabella had passed, Antonio had his whole life planned out. They would have Ashley, move to a bigger house, have another baby, and raise both of them together.

But now that she's gone, all his plans are dead.

Just like she is.

He didn't how to be a father. He was going to learn as he went but he knew he would have made a good father.

Now he also had to be a father and a mother. He didn't know if he would be able to do such a thing. Being a father will be difficult but it was nothing compared to being a mother.

There are things that a girl needs in her life and one of the main one is her mother.

A girl relies on her mother to teach her about compassion, true beauty, relationships, and the importance of life. Some things that a father can also teach but never nearly as well as a mother.

But Ashley's mother is dead.

Antonio heard footsteps approaching him. He slowly looked up and saw Dr. Carson.

Antonio stood up.

There was a little spark of hope inside of him that hoped Isabella was able to be saved but his hopes soon diminished when he saw the regretful and remorseful look on Dr. Carson's face.

"I'm sorry Antonio. We tried our best to revive her but she's gone." his voice was soft. It was if he was scared that he spoke in any other tone, Antonio would break down.

"I see." Antonio replied. His voice was void of any emotions. He turned around and started walking away. His feet dragged him towards the infirmary and he stared through the glass window.

His eyes quickly met with that of his daughter and a soft smile came onto his lips. Her eyes reminded him so much of her mother's and he knew right then and there that he would do anything to protect his little girl.

"Antonio. Here are the files that you have asked for." Antonio's secretary handed him a file and sat down on the sat across from him. She smiled warmly as he took the files out of her hands. "I heard that Ashley is back in town."

Antonio nodded his head and smiled back at her.

"She's been back for the three days now. I haven't seen her in over a decade. It feels so refreshing to have her back with me again." He opened up the files and looked down at it. A frown came onto his lips. "Elena, who signed this contract?"

Elena stood up and walked behind him. Her eyes peered down and her eyebrows furrowed. "I think Rafael did."

"Can you have Martha send Rafael in to meet me later today? These files seem odd." He muttered. His eyes skimmed through the file again. "Who is Dante Hastings?" the name seemed familiar to him but his mind couldn't formulate on who that was.

"He's the owner of Brigsons Law Firm. They never lost a case before. He's known to be an excellent judge of character. If we can get him to become our lawyer, the company would be strongly protected." Elena recited as if it was implanted in her memory for ages.

"Get me an appointment with him as soon as possible. I want to make a deal with him." Antonio closed up the files and handed it back to Elena. He stood up and straightened up his tie. "Thank you Elena."

Elena nodded her head and smiled at him. "It's my job to know these things." she grabbed the files, ignoring the small spark that she received when her hand touched the tip of his finger.

Antonio chuckled. "I didn't mean that." He smiled at her. "I meant thank you for being so loyal to me all of these years. I'm lucky to have you Elena."

Elena nodded her head, a small blush appearing on her face, "Of course." she said softly. "Do you mind if I come over later? I want to see Ashley again. I haven't seen her ever since she was a small child."

Antonio nodded his head. "Why of course you may. You're always welcome."

"Thank you." Elena smiled at him and walked out the door.

Antonio sighed and sat back down on his seat. His eyes wandered to the picture that sat on his desk.

The last picture that he had with Ashley before he had allowed her to go live with her grandparents in the states.

His eyes glossed over with tears as he remembered the many years he lost with her because of his selfish actions.

There's still time left for him to make it up to her. He thought to himself.

He stood up quickly and grabbed all of his documents, putting them into his briefcase. He pressed on the intercom.

"How may I help you Mr. Valldarri?" a voice quickly responded.

"Change my appointment with Rafael to tomorrow and every other ones to next week. I'm heading out for the day." He ordered quickly. He grabbed his coat and put it on, looking at the time.

"Of course Mr. Valldarri. Anything else?"

"Have everyone leave at three today. Spend the day with your family." he smiled and turned off the intercom.

Walking out of the office, he was greeted with shock faces from the whole staff. He nodded his head at them and walked out of the building.

He knew what he had to do.

.

.

.

Ashley walked into the kitchen and sat down on the stool. Her belly made it hard for her to reach the seat but she somehow managed. She took her phone out of her pocket and sighed when she saw the dozen of emails from her friends and co-workers asking where she was.

Only a few people knew that she moved and she knew that she could trust them to keep things silent. She didn't want word to get out that she was in Italy and especially didn't want others to know that she was Antonio Valldarri's daughter.

That would only create trouble for her seeing that he was father owned one of the biggest business in the whole entire world.

She would never be able to get any privacy if word was able to get out. She had already had enough with the public announcement of her and Dante's divorce and she didn't need the paparazzi prying into her life even more.

She didn't want that kind of life for her babies.

A life in which every little thing they did was exposed to the world.

She didn't want them to always be in the center of things. She wanted them to be as safe as they could be. She wanted their lives to remain as private as they would want it too.

Ashley heard the front door opening. She turned her head to the entrance of the kitchen. "Ashley, are you home?"

"Yes Papi. I'm in the kitchen." She replied softly.

Her father's head popped into the kitchen and he smiled softly at her. "How has your day been going figlia?" He walked up and sat down on the stool next to her.

She smiled and shrugged her shoulders. "Same as yesterday."

Antonio chuckled and motioned towards her stomach. "And how are those baminos?"

Ashley placed her hand on her stomach and smiled down at it. "Same as yesterday. Giving their mama a hard time."

He chuckled again. "Just like you did when your mama was this pregnant with you." he said softly. His eyes glossed over with tears and he put his hand on her cheek. "You look so much like her. You have her eyes you know."

Ashley smiled sadly at him. "I know Papi. You told me a million times before."

"I have something for you." He got off the chair. Grabbing her hand, he helped her down and smiled softly. "Come with me."

Ashley furrowed her eyebrows but followed him nonetheless.

"Ah here it is." They stopped at the closet behind the stairs and her eyebrows furrowed even more.

"The closet? You wanted to give me the closet." She asked incredulously.

A chuckle left his mouth and he shook his head. "No bambina. It's what is inside this closet." he took his keys out of his pocket and inserted one of it into the lock. Smiling he opened the door and turned on the light. "Stay here while I find it."

Ashley nodded her head. She leaned her body against the wall and rubbed her belly. "Your nonno is a little crazy isn't he?" she whispered softly to them.

"I heard that young lady!" Antonio shouted from inside the closet. Soon, he came out, holding a black journal in his hand. It was small. About the size of his hands and old with some of the pages ripped. "This was your mother's journal." he whispered.

Ashley took the journal gingerly, afraid of damaging it even further. She felt her eyes watering up and looked up at him. "This was mama's?"

Antonio nodded his head and smiled sadly at her.

"She wrote that while she was pregnant with you. I found it hidden under her pillow after her death. I found it once and asked to read it but she didn't let me. She hid it in a new place every single week. Sometimes in the most obvious place but I could never find it."

Ashley opened the book up slowly and looked down at it. Her eyes met the nice writing of her mother who had dated the first entry. "Thank you papi." she whispered, not looking up from the journal.

"You're welcome figlia." He kissed the top of her head. "Your mother would have been so proud of you." he whispered.

"Papi, I'm a divorced mother. She would never be proud of that." Ashley whispered.

Using his index finger, he pulled her chin up and smiled softly at her. "Your mother will be very proud of you no matter what happens. Just like I am proud of you." he whispered. "I'll leave you to read it now." He turned around and started walking away.

.

.

.

Hope you guys enjoyed that!

Love you all of my lovely owlers!

~Amber <3 <3 <3

Chapter 8

Hello my lovelies. How are you this fine day/night? So here's chapter 8. Sorry I couldnt have posted it sooner. One the bright side. This chapter is 10 pages long on word and 4008 words. Whaaaat?! Longest chap so far or nawh?

In this Chapter, you get to see one of the old character again! Yay! I actually like her a lot this way. Just read and find out ((:

Enjoy!

.

.

.

Chapter 8

Antonio loosened up his tie and opened up the door. His mouth opened to shout out his usual greeting to his wife when he remembered that she was dead and that no one was home. Sighing, he walked over to his couch and sat down on it.

He buried his head into his hands and rubbed his face tiredly. It has been a tough day.

Tougher than usual.

Looking up, he stared at the fireplace mantel where a picture of him and Isabella lies. Walking up to it, Antonio let loose of his tears once again.

He picked it up, his thumb caressing her face softly. "I miss you, mi amor. You have no idea how much I need you right now. Why did you have to leave me so soon?" he whispered. He hugged the picture closely to his chest.

His knees wobbled and he collapsed on the ground. Sobs wrecked his body and he did nothing to stop them.

It's been two months but the feeling was still fresh.

If anything, the feeling only got worse as time drone on. The feeling of the heart getting stabbed so many times but miraculously it still beats.

He would pray to God everyday to take the pain away from him. He didn't want to live this life alone without her. It held no value to him if he didn't have her in this world with him.

She was the love of his life and to have her taken away from him so soon? It's impossible for him to love anyone as much as he loved her.

She was his whole life.

He heard the front door creak open and a voice said softly. "Come on baby. Let's get you into bed shall we? You had such a tiring day today."

Antonio got up from the ground. He kissed the frame and placed it back on the mantel. Only this time, he placed the frame face down, hiding the picture from view. Wiping his tears, he walked towards the voice.

A small tired smile made it's way to his face. "Hello Elena."

Elena smiled sadly back at him and adjusted the sleeping baby in her arms. "Hello Antonio. How was work today?"

"Normal as always." he muttered under his breath but he knew Elena had heard. His eyes zoomed in on the baby. She squirmed slightly and opened up her eyes. Antonio quickly diverted his. "I hope she was no trouble." he muttered.

"Trouble? Little Ashley here? Oh no Antonio. She was such a good girl. Like she always is." Elena said lovingly. She placed a kiss on the baby's head and smiled.

Ashley cooed and tilted her lips into a smile. Her small hands reached out and tugged lightly on Elena's hair.

"Would you like to hold her? She misses her father dearly." Elena muttered softly. She slowly reached Ashley out to Antonio but retreated when she saw the step that Antonio took back. "Antonio," she muttered quickly.

"You should put her to bed, Elena. And head to bed yourself." he said quickly. As quickly as he said that, he made his way into the kitchen and opened up the fridge. He heard Elena coming up from behind him but made no move.

"Antonio, you can't continue like this." Elena whispered. "You have to hold her one day. She already lost her mother, don't make her lose her father also."

"I'm not—" Antonio stopped. He sighed and looked at the baby sleeping in Elena's arms and looked away. "I can't. She reminds me too much of Isabella and what she had to go through." he whispered quickly.

"Antonio, I know it must be so hard for you to lose Isabella but it's even harder for Ashley. She's just a small baby Antonio. She's innocent in all this. Her is still pure and everyday that you spend ignoring her, that purity is just going to keep on fading." Elena turned Antonio's face towards her using her hands and stared into his eyes. "You have to be stronger than this, Antonio."

Antonio pushed her hand away and ignored the hurt look that crossed in her eyes. "You will never understand Elena! You didn't lose the love of your life! I did!" he shouted at her.

A loud cry came out of Ashley's lips as soon as she heard the loudness of his voice. Her eyes instantly filled with tears and her grip on Elena's hair became even stronger. It was to the point of hurting Elena.

Elena didn't pay no mind to the pain. She rocked Ashley slowly. "Sh. It's okay baby. I'm here. I got you." she whispered softly. Her eyes shined brightly with love at Ashley as she started to calm down. "There you go. Who's my good little girl?"

Antonio turned away from the scene and sighed. "I'm sorry. I didn't mean to startle her." he whispered with regret.

Elena turned away from him, not being able to bear the pain that she felt from looking at him. "You may have lost your wife but that's no excuse for your behavior. Grow up. Not everything is about you anymore. You now have an innocent baby relying on you for her every single need."

"I don't appreciate the tone you're using with me Elena." Antonio said harshly. "Remember that you are still my employee and I still have the power to fire you."

"Then why don't you?" Elena hissed out as she turned around. She glared at him and bounced Ashley softly. "Tell me Antonio, why don't you just go ahead and fire me right now?"

Antonio stayed silent. He just stared at her, not knowing what to say. He has never seen Elena so angry before. She was always so calm and always kept her anger at bay. Never has he seen her display such strong anger before.

"Do you know why you won't or can't?" She looked into his eyes and showed him all of the emotions that she felt. Hurt, anger, and disappointment. "You need me Antonio, more than you'll ever know. Without me, you're a lost cause. I'm your only chance at survival."

With that being said Elena walked away, leaving Antonio to deal with his thoughts difficulties on his own.

.

.

.

Antonio woke up the next morning to loud screams, cries, and shouts.

Letting out a groan, he pushed his blanket aside, got up, and walked downstairs to see what all the commotion was all about. Never in the past two months, has he ever heard Ashley cry as much as she was right now.

He sought to find out the cause of her disturbance.

Elena was the first thing he saw he got near.

Then Ashley.

Instead of carrying Ashley like she normally did, Elena stood in the middle of the living room shouting at something or more specifically someone. She glared at the person and walked over to Ashley, who was crying hysterically in her crib.

Picking her up, she instantly started calming the small girl down with hush whispers.

"That girl does not belong here!" an all familiar voice shouted.

A voice that can bring any man to the point of wanting to cut off their ears.

Antonio was so distracted by Ashley that he didn't see her standing there.

Alessandra.

The adopted sister of Isabella.

"This girl has more right to be here more than you ever do." Elena hissed angrily. Up until last night, he had thought that he would only be the only person to be on the receiving end of Elena's anger but currently, he seems to be proven wrong.

Alessandra laughed humorlessly. "That girl is a monster. She killed her own mother." Alessandra glared at Ashley and pointed at her. "She will never belong here. Not when she's a killer."

"She's a baby!" Elena shouted loudly.

Her voice startled Ashley again making Ashley erupt into new cries.

"I'm so sorry baby." she whispered softly into Ashley's ear, gently rocking her. She hugged Ashley closer to her chest and glared at Alessandra. "She is not a monster or is she a killer."

The two ladies seemed to not notice Antonio and that provided a perfect chance for him to sneak away but for some reason, he felt compelled to stay behind. He felt the urge to speak up and protect Ashley and Elena but kept silent.

"How can you say that when the only reason Isabella died was because of that?" Alessandra glared harshly at Ashley. Her hate seemed to never end by the look in her eyes and Antonio instantly feared for what Alessandra can do to Ashley.

"Isabella's death was an accident!" Elena shouted.

"Just like her." The words came out of her mouth and pierced through Antonio's heart painfully. But Alessandra didn't stop there. "She is the result of Isabella's---"

"Enough." Antonio said sharply.

The two women snapped their heads towards him. Alessandra instantly paled while Elena only glanced at him for a second before returning her glare at Alessandra. Clearly, Elena was still mad at him for last night.

"That is enough." his voice was steel cold. He walked over to Elena and took Ashley into his arms, ignoring the shock look on Elena's face as he did so. On instinct, he started to rock her. "You have said enough Alessandra."

"Antonio." she stuttered out.

"I will not tolerate how you treat Elena and Ashley in my house. My daughter," he emphasized, "is no killer and she is definitely not a monster. She might not have been the most expected thing in my life but I love her."

"You can't really be serious right now." her voice held shock and strong repulsion, all directed towards Antonio. "That thing---"

"Her name is Ashley!" he turned towards her and glared harshly. "She is not an object. She is a human being and she is my daughter! And no one will ever disrespect my daughter right in front of me. Ever."

Gasps fell out of Elena's and Alessandra's mouth.

Alessandra because she never would have thought Antonio would have chosen Ashley's side through everything that has happened while Elena because of how proud and happy she was to see Antonio holding his daughter for the first time ever since the girl was born.

"You're making a mistake." Alessandra said coldly once she composed herself. "You are making a huge mistake right now Antonio."

Antonio turned away from her and looked down at Ashley. Somehow, she has managed to fall asleep right in her father's arms.

Antonio smiled softly and caressed her cheek with his thumb. "No, Alessandra. I don't think I am. In fact, I think this has been the best decision that I have ever made."

He started to walk away but paused for a second.

He turned around and gave her a fake smile. "I would say that it was nice you see you again but I would be lying. You know where the door is. You may show yourself out."

He then turned to Elena and gave her a true and genuine smile. "Can you make me a bottle for Ashley?"

Elena nodded her head astonishingly. She then snapped out of her daze and smiled at him.

"Of course. I had it already made but didn't have time to give it to her yet. I'll go heat it up right now." She gave him a proud smile and walked off.

Both of them ignored the loud huff coming from Alessandra and the loud slamming of the door only seconds later.

Antonio continued smiling down at Ashley. "Hello Ashley. If you don't remember who I am, I'm your father. I love you so much. I'm sorry that it took so long for me to figure it out. I was lost and confused once your mother passed away. Before she did, we went through so many rough patches that we were able to overcome. But once she did, I felt my strength leave my whole body. I couldn't look at you clearly without seeing the result of what had happened that day."

Antonio closed his eyes and held back his tears. He opened them again and kissed the top of her head. "I'm so sorry baby girl. I'm so sorry for being such a bad father these past two months. I missed two precious months with you. I promise you now that I will never miss another single part of your life. I promise you this." he kissed the top of her head and sighed deeply.

"I love you babygirl."

.

.

.

Elena walked up to the front door and smoothed out all the wrinkles on her dress. She took the keys out of her pocket and inserted into the lock. She opened the door nervously and poked her head in.

"Hello? I'm here." she opened the door fully and walked inside the house, closing the door behind her.

She saw Ashley at the top of the stairs. Placing her hand over her mouth, Elena felt tears rushing down her eyes when she saw how full grown Ashley looked. "Ashley." she whispered softly. She started walking towards the stairs while tears fell down her face.

"Aunt Elena." she heard Ashley muttering softly.

Once Ashley has reached the bottom of the stairs, Elena engulfed her into a tight hug, being wary of the bump that she saw Ashley carrying on her way down. She pulled away and grabbed Ashley's face into her hands. "Oh you're so grown-up. You look beautiful."

Ashley laughed lightly. Her hand rested on the top of Elena's. "I missed you so much." she whispered, pulling Elena back into a huge. She basked in the sweet and homey smell that Elena seemed to carry constantly with her.

Elena smiled and closed her eyes.

"I missed you too baby." She pulled away again and kissed Ashley's forehead. "It seems just like yesterday you were just in my arms, a newborn, with no experience in the world that surrounds her. Now look at you. All grown up and about to start your own family."

Elena didn't miss the pained look in Ashley's eyes and she didn't miss the fake smile on her face either. She could fool anyone but never will she be able to fool the woman who raised her for her whole childhood. "Something is wrong isn't it?"

Ashley nodded her head and looked at the ground. "I got divorced a few weeks ago." she whispered. "He thought I had cheated on him and that these babies aren't his. He even called them bastard children."

Elena wiped away a lone tear that fell down Ashley's face. She smiled sadly at Ashley. "He doesn't know what he's missing out on. Bella, you're an amazing girl. There will be other guys out there."

Ashley laughed and shook her head. "No man would want a divorce mother of two. There are so many other women out there for them."

Elena scowled at her and smacked Ashley's arm softly. "Don't you dare say that Ashley! Any man will be lucky to have you. Now I heard the word two. Twins?"

Ashley nodded her head and smiled. Her eyes fell down to her stomach and she placed her hand on it. "I'm going to find the genders next month."

Elena smiled and held Ashley's hand. "I'm very happy for you. These babies will be very lucky to have you as their mother. You will make a wonderful mother Ashley. That much I know."

Ashley smiled and hugged her again. "Thank you Elena." she whispered softly.

With Elena there with her, Ashley knew that she could overcome any obstacle that was to be thrown her way. And with the life that she's leading so far, those obstacles will never stop coming.

.

.

.

Ashley looked at Elena and her father and smiled to herself. They seemed to be so comfortable with each other. The way that her father smiled so softly and so freely around Elena just shows how much he is smitten by her.

The way that Elena would stare at her father from time to time with a distant look in her eye shows just how much she yearned to be with him.

Ashley cleared her throat and smiled to herself when she saw the disappointed look in their eyes.

"I'm going to head to my room now. These babies are taking the energy out of their mother." she chuckled and stood up with a smile on her face. "Thank you for coming today Elena. I hope to see you around more often."

Elena nodded her head at Ashley, smiling widely. "Of course. I'm going to be around more than you think I am."

Ashley opened her mouth to speak up but shut it when she heard the doorbell go off. She excused herself and walked towards the front door. She grabbed a napkin off the side table and wiped her hands.

Opening the door there was a smile on her face but it dropped as soon as it came face to face with the last person she wanted to see.

"Alessandra." she whispered.

Alessandra gave her a smirk and walked in the house, purposely bumping into Ashley's shoulder. "Oh excuse me. Ashley dear you mustn't stand in the way like that."

Ashley closed the door and looked at her. "What are you doing here?" she asked. She placed her hand on her stomach protectively. "Papa told me you didn't live here anymore."

Alessandra laughed and flipped her platinum blonde hair over her shoulder. No matter how old Alessandra got, she seemed to be looking ten years younger than her actual age.

A trait that made Alessandra more confident than she should be.

"Ashley, figlia, who's at the---Alessandra." her father spat out the name like it was venom to his vocal cords.

"Oh! Antonio how good to see you again darling!" Alessandra said cheerfully.

"I wish I can say to same to you."

Ashley turned her head and saw Elena standing next to Antonio with her arms crossed over her chest. The fun and peaceful atmosphere that was there only minutes ago instantly disappeared with tension and foreboding replacing it.

"My my my. Seems to be an endless amount of reunions today." Alessandra smiled fakely. "Elena how good to see you again. Oh is that a gray hair on your head dear?" she tsked. "You stress too much. It's not good you know? Makes you look older than you actually are."

"I don't want small talks Alessandra. What do you want?" Elena demanded instantly shutting down Alessandra's comment.

"I just wanted to see my husband—"

"Ex-husband." Antonio corrected her.

Alessandra waved her hand as if swatting away his comment like she was a fly. "Labels labels labels. Don't like them. Never did."

"I won't ask again Alessandra. What do you want?" Elena glared at her. "If you don't have an answer then leave and don't come back. Ever."

Alessandra finally let go of her fake cheery. Now a dark woman replaced her. "I want Samuel to be able to move back into this house. He has done nothing wrong."

Elena instantly shook her head and glared even harder at her. "Are you crazy? Your pathetic excuse of a son is not going anywhere near Antonio or Ashley."

"He will move back in here!" Alessandra shouted as her hands started making crazy motions around her.

Ashley instantly moved back from her and covered her stomach with her arm. She looked at her father and saw him staring at her in worry at the close proximity of Alessandra to her. She moved to the side and started to walk backwards to her father.

Once she felt his hand on her arm, she sighed in relief.

"Over my dead body." Elena hissed out.

"That can be arranged." A smile full of malice and destruction locked itself on Alessandra;s lips. "You don't understand dear Elena. You don't have a choice." Alessandra turned to Ashley and smiled wickedly. "I see you're pregnant. How wonderful."

Ashley held her head up and stared blankly at Alessandra. "Yes. What's it to you?" her voice was monotone and dry. Ashley didn't feel like wasting her energy to put any kind of emotion towards this woman.

"It would be a shame if anything happened to those babies wouldn't?" There was a gleeful look in her eyes as she said that.

Ashley instantly felt her father pushing her back. But she could still see Alessandra over her father's shoulder. "You wouldn't." she whispered. Her arm wrapped around her stomach even tighter trying to shield her babies away from harm.

"Oh would I?" Alessandra taunted.

"You cruel bitch." Elena hissed out. "Have you no morals at all that you're willing to kill innocent children just for your own sick pleasure?"

Alessandra laughed loudly humorlessly. "Innocent? You forgot who their mother is. Ashley is the reason why Isabella is dead. Why? Because of the one mistake that Isabella had made that winter night."

Ashley felt shock shaking through her whole body. She backed away and looked at Alesandra. She gulped. "What are you talking about?"

"Oh Antonio! You didn't tell her? Allow me!" Alessandra giggled gleefully.

Antonio looked at Ashley desperately. "Go to your room please."

Ashley shook her head and looked at him with hurt in her eyes. "Papi what is she talking about? What does she mean by momma made a mistake?"

"Well that's what she did dearie!" Alessandra said in a singsong voice. "She made a mistake. A big mistake."

"Papa." Ashley whispered.

"Ashley please go up to your room." Elena pleaded from the side.

"Oh out with it already!" Alessandra smiled and for once, it was one that was filled with no malice. "You see Ashley, you were never suppose to happen. Your mother made a mistake and you were the result. You aren't a true Valldarri. You're just a mistake that your mother gave to your father to live with."

As soon as that was said, Ashley's whole world turned black.

.

.

.

Dante looked up as a file was dropped loudly on his desk. Seeing that it was Thomas, Dante grabbed the file and opened it up. "What is this?" He read the first three lines and looked up again. "Antonio Valldarri?"

Thomas grinned and sat down across from him. "Biggest Hotel owner currently in all of Europe. If we can get him to be one of clients, our firm will grow so much more."

"What do we have to do?" Dante asked. He closed the file and slid it back to Thomas. Leaning back against his chair, he folded his hands together.

"What do you have to do." Thomas corrected.

"Me?"

Thomas grinned widely. "All you have to do is go to Italy, meet with him, have lunch or dinner with his family, impress him somehow, and the deal is ours."

"That's all I have to do?" Dante stood up and straightened his tie.

"Yes. And to help you get over Ashley, I heard Valldarri has a daughter who recently just moved back to Italy. Soften her up somehow and done deal." Thomas stood up also and walked towards the door. "Think about it for a little while. The plane leaves in three days. Either you go or I will go. Much preferred to be you though."

Dante nodded his head. "I'll go." he looked out his window as Thomas walked out of the room. Dante sighed and pressed his hand against the glass.

"I miss you Ashley." he whispered.

.

.

.

WHAT ALESSANDRA?!?! NO WAY!!! Yeah I like her actually. Her craziness makes me so happy. Everyone is all sad and depressed and then there's Alessandra. So confident and so crazy and delusional and twisted. Ooooh. I love her. haha!

Hope you guys enjoyed!

Love you all of my lovely owlers!

~Amber <3 <3 <3

Chapter 9

- -

Hello there beautiful and amazing people. Sorry that it took me almost a whole month to get this chapter up! I'm trying my best, I swear. Also, I don't know why but I have not been able to open any of my messages lately. Reporting the problem to wattpad right now! Anyways.. .Enjoy guys!

Chapter 9

Ashley took a seat on the bench and stared straight ahead of her. Her lips curved up into a smile as she watched the kids play with each other happily. Warmth flew into her heart as the kids treated each other with equal respect.

A little girl fell down as she chased after a boy.

Ashley stood up to go help her but stopped.

A group of kids ran towards the little girl and began to baby her.

The boy she was chasing ran up to her with a worried expression. He knelt down next to her and began to look for injuries.

A small laugh escaped Ashley's lips when the small girl just pushed him away.

Without anybody's help, the girl stood up on her own, and told them that she was fine. As to prove her point, the little girl touched the boy's shoulders and ran away, laughing as she went.

Ashley felt a presence sitting down next to her. She didn't need to turn to see who it was. She already knew.

"Why are you here?" Her voice was monotonous while her whole body straightened up and starting to build a defense stance.

"That little girl reminds me so much of you. Always independent and standing on your own two feet." he said softly, ignoring her question.

"I didn't agree to this meeting for small talks. I'm going to ask you again. Why are you here and what do you want?" She turned to him and glared at him. "I don't like wasting my time and that's exactly what you're doing."

"Alright. I'll tell you." he sighed and smiled softly at her. "I wanted to apologize for the way I had treated you when we were little kids. It was wrong of me to do so."

Ashley quickly turned away as he said that and returned her gaze to the group of kids. "Don't you think it's a little too late for that?"

"I need to let you know something. It's not going to be easy for you or for me but I have kept it inside of me for too long. You deserve to know the truth. If you need or even want, I can be your shoulder to cry on." he took a deep breath.

Ashley scoffed. "You're delusional to think I would lean on you."

He sighed.

"Just tell me what you need to and leave." she whispered.

"It's not easy."

Ashley knew based on his tone that whatever he had to say was unutterable. She prepared herself for the worst. Closing her eyes, she prayed that she'll still remain sane after this visit. She opened her eyes. "What is it Samuel?"

"I'm your brother. Your half-brother to be exact. I'm not just your brother through marriage but I'm also your brother through blood."

The words instantly made Ashley freeze. Her whole mind started to only focus on what he had just told her. The world was caving in on her and she fought hard to breathe. Clutching her fists around her handbag, she started to hyperventilate.

"Crap. Ashley, are you okay?" he stood in front of her and grab her shoulders with worry clear in his eyes. "Ashley! Can you hear me? Answer me please. Say something." He himself started to shake.

"No. No you're lying." Ashley responded. She stood up and slapped him across the cheek. "You are just trying to get under my skin. Well guess what Samuel? It worked."

Samuel shook his head violently. He grabbed her arms and held it softly. His eyes shone with unshed tears. "Ashley I'm not. Please believe me."

She yanked her arms out of his hand. Poking his chest harshly she said, "Don't think I don't know what you're up to Samuel. Elena told me that you and your mother got kicked out of my father's house."

Once again, he shook his head. "This has nothing to do with that Ashley, I swear. I don't care about that. All I want is to reconcile with you."

Ashley saw the genuine look in his eyes but told herself that he was just acting. It was all just a game to him and his mother. She scoffed and tears started to fall down violently. "Haven't you destroyed my life enough, Samuel?"

"Ashley please just hear me out." Samuel pleaded.

Shaking her head and laughing emotionlessly, she turned her face away from him. "You took my childhood away."

"I didn't know. Had I known—"

"It doesn't matter Samuel! Whether or not I was your blood related sister, you still should not have treated me that way. You made me become insecure. You made me feel like no one would ever love me." she wiped away her tears and looked back at him. "I never want to see you again. Don't contact me ever."

"Ashley wait please." There was tears also falling down his cheeks. His face looked at her with an emotion that she has never seen before.

"Good-bye Samuel." she whispered. "Please. Let me live my life in peace. It's good where it's at right now. I have a good husband and a good mindset. Let me be happy. For once."

"I can't Ashley. I—I need to make up for my past mistakes." He grabbed her hand again and looked at her with sadness. "Please, don't go."

She yanked her hand and walked away from him, not looking back. Ignoring the calls from him, she picked up her phone and called her husband.

It took a few seconds before he picked up.

Her heart fluttered in happiness when she heard his voice. "Hey. I need to tell you something tonight. Try to come home early, okay?" she hung up the phone and smiled.

Forcing herself to forget the encounter with Samuel, she made her way home. As she passed by the houses in the neighborhood, her hand reached towards her stomach and rubbed it. "Let's do this my babies."

.

.

.

Ashley slowly opened her eyes and sat up on her bed. She felt a slight pain on her lower abdomen but dismissed it as nothing. She had worst pains than those. Her doctor told her that it was more or less normal.

The conversation from before she passed out replayed in her mind. Questions started to drill their way into her head. Disbelief was the only feeling that consumed her body at the moment. That and a feeling of betrayal like always.

She heard her door opening and already knew who it was. "What did she mean down there, Elena?"

Ashley didn't look at her. She was afraid of the truth that could already be shining through Elena's eyes.

"I'm not the person to tell you this." Elena muttered.

Ashley felt the end of her bed dipping softly. "Then who is?"

It was silence for a while. Ashley debated against herself if she could ask it again. But before she could, Elena answered her. "That book on your nightstand."

Ashley grabbed the book and finally turned to Elena. Elena didn't meet her eyes. "What does my mama's journal have anything to do with this?"

"It will answer everything. That book was your mother's best friend. Your father didn't just give you the journal to help you go through with your pregnancy. It was to also tell you the truth." Elena finally looked up. "The darkest secrets that your mama ever had is in that very journal. All you have to do it open it."

"Will it answer every single question I have?" Ashley whispered.

Elena nodded her head. "Just promise me something."

"What?" Ashley muttered. Turning the book over, she caressed the cover and started to prep herself to read.

"Promise me that no matter what you read in there, you won't think negatively of your mother." Elena placed her hand on Ashley's. "Promise me Ashley."

"I promise."

.

.

.

For hours, Ashley spent just staring at the journal. Brown leather with a strap on it. A strap that she couldn't bring herself to open.

The journal just laid there, on her bed, calling out for her to open it. The neat handwriting on the front cover stating who it belonged to made Ashley only fear it even more.

Hands reached out, mind set, and her breath evened out, Ashley picked it up. She commanded herself to open it but her hands wouldn't move itself toward the strapped. Frozen it stayed, her thumb on the front cover while her other four fingers on the back.

"You know, staring at it all day won't let you know the truth."

Ashley let out a small screech and her hand let go of the book.

It flew all the way across the room and she cringed when she heard the clank as it met with the floor. Praying that it hadn't gotten damaged, she got off her bed and walked to it. She picked it up and sighed in relief.

Eyes burning with fury, she turned towards the intruder.

"You scared me."

"It's a habit." he smirked and leaned his body against the door. "Well?"

"Well what?" she snapped out.

"My, my, someone is not a happy camper today." Laughing he loosened his tie and rolled his sleeves up.

"What do you want?" Placing the book back on her nightstand, Ashley sat down on her bed. "Can't you see I'm busy."

"Totally. Because staring at the same journal for the past four hours is totally being busy. My, Ashley. You're such a productive person." He let out a chuckle and walked towards the edge of her bed, sitting on it. He smiled softly at her. "I just missed you."

Ashley smiled back at him. She scooted towards him and hugged him tightly. "I missed you too Frankie, my annoying little cousin."

"By four days." he scoffed and poked her cheek. Seriousness then took over his eyes again. "You may seem okay but I know you're not." he leaned his head on hers and wrapped his arm around her shoulder. "You want to tell me all about what's going on?"

Ashley smiled sadly at him and just shook her head. "Another time. I just want to forget everything for now. These babies are my main focus right now."

Frankie nodded his head and kissed her forehead softly. "If you ever need me, I'm just a few room down." he smirked.

Ashley raised her eyebrows at him. "You're staying here."

Smirking he flicked her forehead softly. "Of course I am. Someone has to stay here and protect you when Samcow starts to live here."

Ashley felt her whole body freeze. "Samuel? He's coming here?" she whispered.

Frankie sighed. "Yeah I know. Uncle Antonio did try but Ursula down there got him to agree somehow."

Ashley laughed. "Her name is Alessandra."

"Right I knew that." Frankie laughed and stood up. He kissed her forehead again. "I'll see you at dinner in a bit."

She smiled back at him. "Alright."

He sighed dramatically. "Wish me luck. I'm about to go meet Morgana again."

"Alessandra." She corrected again.

"Oh. Cool."

.

.

.

Hm...Who do you guys think that person is? So many options right guys? haha not really. There's only three people so far that is not related to Ashley by blood. So they're your only choices RIGHT NOW on who is that mysterious person.

Hope you guys enjoyed that! any confusion, feel free to comment it and I will get back to you as past as possible!

Love you all of my lovely owlers!

~Amber <3 <3 <3

Chapter 10

I don't really like this chapter much to be honest but oh wells. I'm trying my best to update regularly guys, I swear but it's awfully hard right now. So I do apologize if I can't update any time soon.

Anyways, hope you guys enjoy this chap despite it's choppiness.

.

.

.

Chapter 10

Samuel looked down at the little girl.

A small smile light up her face when she saw him but he made no motion to smiling back.

All he did was just give him a simple blank look before looking up at the man beside her. He knew of the importance that this man is holding over his life now. For now, he and his mother were dependent on this man.

"Antonio." His mother greeted the man with a kiss on the cheek.

"Alessandra," the man responded.

She looked down at Samuel with a smile, love shining in her eyes. "This is Samuel as you have already know." She combed through his hair softly and turned back to the man. "I hope you will be able to treat him with the same love as you do with your biological children."

He had missed the bitter tone in his mother's voice and miss the frown that made a nest on the man's face.

But what he didn't miss was the way the girl looked at his mother with fear shining in her eyes.

He instantly detested her.

The man nodded his head and knelt down, becoming eye to eye with Samuel. "How old are you son?"

"Thirteen." Samuel replied quietly.

The man smiled softly at him and brought the girl forward. She tried to move behind her father's legs but he kept her in front. She kept her head downcast.

"Ashley." The man said in a warning tone.

"Hello." she looked up and looked back down again, not meeting anybody's eyes.

"She sure has grown since the last I've seen her." his mother said. Samuel looked up at his mother and saw hatred swirling in those eyes of her. A feeling that he has never seen on her face. "So much like her mother."

"She has inherited nothing from her father." Antonio joked but Samuel could hear the bitterness that seeped through.

"Hm."

Samuel looked back at the girl again and he grimaced.

She was too shy.

This is going to be easier than he had expected.

"Why don't I show you your rooms?"

"Please."

Samuel walked alongside his mother as they walked into the grand house. Samuel has never been in a place such like this and he looked around the place with awe. Excitement coursed through his veins at the discoveries that he could make in this house.

"Ashley, why don't you show Samuel his room while I give Alessandra a tour of the house." he had the man say softly to the girl.

"Yes papi." she replied back obediently. She turned to Samuel. "Follow me, please." she said meekly.

Samuel rolled his eyes, grabbed his bag from his mother, and followed the girl. They walked up a spiral staircase and Samuel had to urge to reach out and push the girl down the stairs. He held himself back though.

"You're annoying." he blurted out.

"Sorry." she blushed and turned away from him. Her pigtails, slightly whacking him against his face.

"Your hair!" he groaned out loud.

She pulled her pigtails to the front and looked at him with fear. "I'm sorry!" she whimpered and cowered back.

"Whatever." he muttered back. He continued to follow her as she lead him to a room.

"This is yours."

He pushed her aside, though softly, and walked into the room. His eyes brightened when he saw how perfect it was.

Dropping his bags to the floor, he jumped on his bed and grinned. He turned to the door and saw the girl and for once, he didn't feel any negative feelings towards her. "Want to jump on the bed with me?"

She looked at him with surprised for a second. Looking around, she shrugged her shoulders and jumped onto the bed also. The two children started to jump on the bed, laughing happily every time they were in the air.

Samuel grinned happily, already knowing that his new life is going be great. He turned to the girl again but frowned when he saw the large bruise that was on her back. He was tempted to reach out and touch it but held himself back and ignored it.

He doesn't have to care about her. She is nothing to him.

.

.

.

Samuel dropped his bags on the front porch and sighed heavily.

Digging his hands into his pocket, he stared at the house in which he spent most of his teen years. His hands reached out and felt the soft texture of the wooden door and smelt the clean air that was cleansed by the many bushes of roses that surrounded the house.

"Home sweet home." he muttered to himself.

He took a plant to the side and knelt down. On the floor laid a number pad. Putting in the numbers that he memorized by heart, the pad opened up and revealed the key.

He took the key out of the pad and closed it back up, putting the pot back to where it belonged. Pushing the key in and turning it, he opened up the door and smelt the house. He smiled softly to himself and walked in.

He was not expecting a warm welcome at all and was not surprised to see that no one greeted him as he walked in. He sighed sadly, grabbed his bags from the porch and made his way up to his old room.

As he walked in, he placed his bags at the end of his bed and threw himself down. Groaning, he took out his phone and texted his mom telling her that he has arrived.

Looking around the room, he sighed in relief when he saw that nothing has changed and everything was still as neat as when he had left it.

"So you're back."

He turned to the door and smiled softly at him. "Yeah. I don't plan on staying long. I don't want to be a bother or cause any trouble."

Antonio nodded his head. "Listen Samuel, I don't have a problem with you as of right now. But if you treat my daughter similarly to how you treated her when you were kids, I will not hesitate to kick you out of my house."

Samuel shook his head. "I know the truth, Antonio." he muttered.

Antonio didn't look surprised. All he did was just raise his eyebrows. "You know? Who told you?" He sat down at Samuel's desk chair and stared at him.

No emotions were displayed.

"My father. I visited him in prison a few years back. He told me the truth."
Samuel laughed emotionlessly. "The bastard even laughed in my face and
told me how happy he was to ruin the family."

Samuel didn't miss Antonio clenching his fist nor did he miss the hurt look
on Antonio's face.

Samuel sighed and looked away from him. He knew that it was hurting
Antonio to see him right now.

Samuel reminded him too much of the man who took everything away
from him. Of the man who was the root of every single problem that
Antonio had to endure for the past two decades.

"How does the truth change anything though?" Antonio muttered, closing
his eyes and leaning back against the chair.

"She's my sister. I'm her older brother. It's my job to protect her." Samuel
said quietly. He grabbed his bag and started to unpack it. "I saw her a few
years ago. Right after I found out the truth. I thought it was a sign for me
to make amends with her."

Antonio instantly snapped his eyes opened and looked at Samuel with
shock in his eyes. "Ashley knows?"

Samuel smiled sadly again and shook his head. "No. She doesn't believe me.
I don't blame her. Who would want to believe that the person they thought
was their father turns out not to be? Not me."

Antonio sighed and looked down at the ground. "I'd prefer for you to not
bring it up. I want her to find out everything through her mother's journal.
It's the only way for her to not jump to conclusions."

Although Samuel knew it was hard for him to do that he still nodded his head and smiled at Antonio. "I promise I won't bring it up unless she asks me."

Antonio stood up and nodded his head. "That's all I ask for. Thank you."

As Antonio started to walk out the door, Samuel stopped him. "Antonio wait." he called out. He saw Antonio stopping and took a deep breath. "I know it was hard for you to do but I just want to thank you. Thank you for letting me come back despite everything that I have done."

"I didn't do it for you." Antonio said before walking away.

Samuel sighed and pushed his bag to the side again. He got up from the bed and started to walk down the hall to where he knew Ashley was. He stayed outside her door and glanced in, seeing her staring at a book.

"Hey." he muttered quietly as to not scare her.

"I didn't think it would be this quick." she responded back, not glancing up at him. Her face still remained blank, not displaying a single emotion to how she really felt about him moving back in. "I thought I'd have more time."

"I heard you were pregnant." he smiled at her even though she couldn't see it. "Congratulations. You must be excited."

"Not as excited as I am scared." Her eyes snapped up and she smiled sadly at him. "You must have heard the other news also then."

"I have and I'm sorry." Samuel looked at her.

"It's not your fault. You didn't tell him to divorce me." Ashley chuckled emotionlessly. "I actually thought he wanted these babies. Only now do I realized that he cared more for his reputation than he ever did for me."

"You don't really mean that." Samuel said softly.

She shook her head and just continued to smile on as if nothing bad has happened. "No, I don't. I know he did want these babies. He's just too blinded by the lies that people are feeding to him. I know he still loves me."

Samuel walked over to her bed and sat down on it. He didn't miss the way she had stiffened nor did he miss the fear that came into her eyes. A pang tugged at his heart and he tried his best to not show how hurt he was by her actions.

He deserved it anyways.

"Do you know what gender they are?"

"Girls." She responded, a ghost of a smile on her lips. "I have their names already picked out also."

"You do?"

She nodded her head and turned to him, smiling. "Isabella after my mother and Arabella to go with her sister's name."

"They're beautiful names." He smiled at her and leaned back against her headboard. "How long until you're due?"

"Four more months." It was silent for a few seconds.

Samuel could feel her gaze on the side of his head so he turned to her. "What's on your mind right now?"

"If I let you in, will you promise to help me through this?" she whispered vulnerably.

He nodded his head and pulled her into a hug. His chin rested on the top of her head. "I promise. You don't have anything to fear anymore. I promise to protect you from now on. Nothing will hurt you again. Especially me." He kissed the top of her head.

Soft sobs were heard coming from Ashley and all he did to comfort her was rub her back and constantly kiss the top of her head. "I promise." he whispered.

.

.

.

Love you all of my lovely owlers!

~Amber <3 <3 <3

Chapter 11

Hello guys! SORRY FOR POSTING THIS SO LATE! My schedule have been pretty hectic lately. I promise to try to get the next one up asap. No promises though. With that said, enjoy.This is not edited by the way so sorry for any mistakes. ...Chapter 11

"Ciao, mio figlio." Lorenzo greeted. He sat down across from Samuel and ignored the guards cuffing his hand to the table. "I see you have grown into a successful young man."

"Cut the crap, Lorenzo. What do you want?" Samuel stood up and walked towards the door. He leaned against the wall and stared at his father. No. Not father. Sperm donor.

Lorenzo shook his head and chuckled. He leaned back against the seat and smirked. "Why must you always assume that I want something? Can I not see my only son?"

Samuel felt anger course inside of him. He walked towards the table and slammed his hand down on it. The noise echoed loud and made Lorenzo wince. "I know you. I know you always want something. And news flash Lorenzo, you are not my father."

"Then what do you call the person whose blood run through your very own veins. The man who gave you life?"

"A sperm donor. A mistake. An abomination. I despise the blood that runs through my veins. If I could, I would spill every single drop until there is no trace of you inside of me." Samuel hissed out.

"I never knew you felt so strongly about that." Lorenzo looked deep into Samuel's eyes. "Have you no love for the man that gave you life?"

"None."

"I see." Lorenzo looked towards the guard and nodded his head.

The guard came in and uncuffed him. He placed Lorenzo's hands behind his back and started to steer him away.

"Did you call me here just to waste my time?" Samuel said.

"No. I called you here because I missed my son. But clearly, he died long ago." Lorenzo muttered before walking away with the guard.

"Stop."

The guard held Lorenzo back.

"What is it?" Lorenzo said coldly, not looking back.

"I want this to be the last call you ever give me. I want you to never contact me or my family ever again. If I see you near any of them, I will not hesitate to tell Antonio the truth." Samuel sat back down on the chair, not looking at the man whose blood run in his veins.

"Very well. I wish you the best of luck."

Those were the last words that Samuel ever heard from his father. And it was the last time that he saw his father alive. ...

Samuel held Ashley's hands in his own and looked down at the little notebook on her lap.

He picked it up and turned it over, looking at the engravings on it. His hands tenderly ran through the engravings and he smiled to himself.

As he looked up at Ashley, a small smile made its way to his face when he saw her fast asleep.

He placed the journal on her night stand and stood up. Standing up, he pulled the covers up to her chin and kissed her forehead softly. A chuckle left his lips when her hands reached out and clutched tightly to a pillow, murmuring incoherent words.

He walked out of the room, a happy smile on his face, and started to walk towards the kitchen.

A hand reached out and slapped him across his face.

Shocked by the hit, Samuel staggered back and bumped his head into the corner of the cabinet.

Spots filled his vision and he held onto the counter. His head started to throb painfully as his eyes tried to push past the blurriness.

His hand went up to his cheek and glared towards the person that he barely made out. "What was that for?"

"You cannot come back here and ruin Ashley's life." a familiar voice shouted. A finger poked at his chest and probed deep into his skin.

His vision cleared up and he glared at Elena. "I'm not here to ruin her life. I'm here to protect her from the bastard that left her."

Elena scoffed and rolled her eyes. She smacked him across the back of his head. "Don't you dare lie to me, mister. I know that you're only here to make her life more miserable. Her life is bad enough as it is. She doesn't need you to come back in it and ruin it even more."

"She's my sister! I would never hurt her." he defended. He stalked forward, a feeling of superiority passed through him as Elena started stepping backwards. "She is my sister Elena, and I will protect her until the day I die."

"Stop your lies, Samuel." Elena stared deep into his eyes. "I will not stand by and watch her get hurt. I will tolerate you for now but if I see you treating her any different than the way she deserves to be treated, I will not hesitate to kill you. I am willing to do whatever it takes to keep her safe and happy."

"Well, i guess we can agree on one thing then." he replied coldly before leaving the kitchen.

As he walked up the stairs, he felt a feeling of pain tugging at his heart. He was not accepted here, he knows that, but with everything he had in him, he wishes that he would.

His whole life, there were rarely any times where people accepted him. Ashley was the only one who did the moment she saw him but he only hurt her and pushed her away. A decision that he would regret for the rest of his life.

She was his sister and he had hurt her. Hurt the one person who was there for him in his darkest times.

Who, despite his ill treatment towards her, still cared for him. He knew that she hated him when they were kids but also couldn't help caring for him. It was the same for him except she didn't let that hatred consume her and drive her actions while he did.

He passed by Antonio's office but stopped in his tracks when he heard Antonio call for him.

Turning into the office, Samuel looked at Antonio.

The strong urge to make Antonio proud of him was strong. Samuel hated his father and the only close thing he ever had to a father was Antonio.

But he knows that Antonio would never be proud of him. Nobody ever would.

"Yes, Antonio?" Samuel asked with a monotonous voice.

"I have a meeting today with a lawyer from America. I would like for you to come with me and learn some techniques." Antonio pulled the papers together and placed them in a file. He looked up at Samuel and raised his eyebrows. "Or is your schedule not free?"

Samuel shook his head. "No I can go. May I ask why though? You have never interested me with your affairs before."

Antonio continued to look at him with no expression displayed on his face. "Seeing as Ashley cannot run my company any time soon, I would like you hand it over to you when I retire."

Shock coursed through Samuel's body. He pointed to himself and uttered, "Me?"

Antonio crossed his arm over his chest and leaned back against his chair. "Is there anyone else in here besides you Samuel?"

Samuel shook his head, still feeling shocked. "Why would you hand it to me? You hate me."

Antonio shook his head. "I don't hate you Samuel. Dislike? Yes. But not hate. I also know that you are capable of doing this and that you're trying to change yourself to be a better brother to Ashley. I want to give you this chance to prove yourself to be worthy of being in my family."

"I don't know what to say." Samuel muttered. "Antonio, I'm really sorry for any trouble my mother and I have caused to you and Ashley. I was blinded by jealousy."

"What were you jealous of?"

"Ashley. She had a father. Someone I had always wanted to have. I saw how you looked at her. It was a look that my father has never given me before. When he looks at me, all I can see is disgust and hatred." Samuel poured out his heart to Antonio.

He knew that there was no point in hiding his reasons now. It's time for him to be honest to those who he cared about.

"You know that's not true. In his own sick and twisted way, Lorenzo did care for you." Antonio clapped his hand against Samuel's back.

"That's not true."

"He called me on his deathbed. He apologized for what he has done to our family. Though the words did nothing to fix what was already done, I forgave him. And you should also."

For the first time in forever, Samuel saw a smile on Antonio's face.

But not just any smile. It was a smile directed towards him, and only him.

The realization of that caused a surge of happiness to fill his whole body. Right then and there, he swore to himself that he would never let Antonio down ever again. He has done so much without having too.

"Do you really believe I can do it?" Samuel asked, looking down at the ground.

"I don't believe, Samuel. I know." Antonio sat back down on his chair again and looked at the files.

"Please go get ready. We leave for the company soon." Though his voice was stern and demanding, Samuel could still hear the smile in his voice.

Samuel grinned and saluted him. "Yes sir. I swear, I won't disappoint you."

"I know you won't." ...They told me that I would be okay again. Told me that I would be able to move past this. That time will heal everything that I have felt.

But they are wrong. I will never heal from this. The physical wounds, they will heal but will always leave behind a reminder. The emotions that had consumed me will remain and the fear will never leave me.

Those were the first two paragraphs that Ashley had encountered in the journal. She closed the book after and started to pant.

Her heart raced in her chest and she grabbed on her nightstand. She stood but sat back down when a searing pain hit her stomach. Her hands clutched onto it and she winced in pain.

Her eyes started to blur and her heart continued to race even faster. Fear coursed through her brain. She opened her mouth to call out.

To anyone.

To anything.

But no matter how hard she tried, the only sound that came out were her inconsistent panting and gasps. Tears flooded her already blurred eyes.

She clutched the bed sheets, her knuckles starting to also hurt from the force. She closed her eyes shut and tried to call out for someone again.

"Papa." She shouted.

A scream left her lips as another searing pain went through.

"Samuel!"

She continued to scream out their names.

"Elena! Frankie!"

She fisted the sheets with one hand, and with the other, clutched her stomach tightly. She began to pray that there was nothing wrong with her babies. She would never be able to live another day if something were to happen to them.

"Ashley!"

She heard a voice shouting before everything went black. The last thought in her mind was, "Please take me and not my babies." ...Please don't kill me. I'm too young to die. Anyways, i hope you guys had an amazing Christmas and a happy new year! Thank you so much for putting up with me. Love you guys.

Love you all of my lovely owlers! ~Amber <3 <3 <3

Chapter 12

Aye guys! I is back! Sorry for taking so long lately. My life has been very hectic lately but I'm trying my best. Anyways, for anyone who does not understand what's going on, just comment a question on what you don't understand and I'll address it in the following chapters. Hopefully that will help you understand it better. You can even ask me random ass hell questions. ((: My goal is to finish this book soon before summer starts. Let's see how we can get this done. With that being said, enjoy!

.

.

.

Chapter 12

Dante opened his eyes and smiled down at his wife. He held her tighter against his chest. burying his head into her neck.

His heart swelled with love and happiness. He kissed the base of her neck before removing his arms. He did so slowly to prevent her from waking up.

But his efforts were pointless as she made a small groan. Her eyes opened and twinkled like stars in the sky. She rolled the covers off her body, revealing her sun-kissed skin to him.

He felt that familiar tightening down his lower region and groaned. His eyes caught her mischievious glint and he glared at her. He knew that she wasn't going to let him ravish her so early in the morning so he opted for the bathroom. "You're cruel."

A laugh sounded in the air making Dante's sour expression turn into a soft smile. He walked back to her and kissed her forehead softly. "I love you."

"Love you too." She muttered back before kissing his cheek softly.

He felt her soft skin against his and fought the urge to push her down on the bed and take her until she couldn't remember her own name. "Go put on a robe before we're both late for work."

She laughed and moved away from him. Pulling his t-shirt over her head, she winked. "Good enough for me."

She gave him a sly smile and walked out of the room, swaying her hips from side to side.

Dante groaned again, his eyes darted to the bathroom. Time for another cold shower, like every morning. ..."I see you are finally dressed." Dante leaned against the doorframe and crossed his arm over his chest. His eyes zoomed in on her rear and a rumble of satisfaction left him.

"I wouldn't want the neighbors seeing what is clearly taken." She said cheekily, landing him a wink.

"Good because you're all mine." He walked up to her and wrapped his arms around her waist. He pulled her back against his chest and smiled at her flipping the pancakes.

"Pancakes again?" He muttered, kissing her neck.

She moaned and leaned her neck to the side, giving him more access. "What we want, we get."

He pushed his hand up and left it on her stomach. "Is she treating you okay?"

"He is treating me just fine." She laughed.

"He?" Dante turned her around and smirked. "No darling. It's a she."

Ashley shook her head at him and stuck her tongue out. "My body, my prediction."

Dante chuckled and kissed her cheek. He looked at the time and sighed in disappointment.

"I'm sorry, baby." He said, grabbing her hand.

She gave him a confused look but she frowned when she saw the guilty look on his face. "You're skipping breakfast again?"

Dante nodded his head and pulled her against his chest. "I'm sorry. I have to be early today. The merger needs more work."

She pulled away from him.

He felt a clench in his chest knowing that she was upset.

Her face was turned away from his.

He pulled her chin up and looked into her eyes. "You know, once the merger is over with, I'll have all the time in the world with you."

"Sure." She muttered. She sighed and smiled at him. "I guess I'll just have lunch with you later today after the appointment."

Dante's eyes widened. "What appointment?"

Ashley narrowed her eyes at him. "The one that's today."

"That's today? Crap."

Ashley's eyes filled with hurt. "You forgot about the appointment? Dante you promised me."

Dante slid his hand down his face. "It's just I have an appointment with the Brooklyn's about the merger. Constantine said they won't reschedule."

"The same one who's been trying to sleep with you for months?" Ashley shook her head and pushed him away. "Forget it. I can just go by myself."

"Ashley-"

"No Dante. Just go to your stupid meeting." She muttered.

Dante sighed. He looked at her for a second before grabbing his briefcase. He walked out the door but he didn't miss the lone tear that slid down her cheek.

It took all he had to not go back there and take the day off. But if he was to provide for his family, he has to get this merger. ...Dante stepped out of the airport and breathed in the Italian air. A sense of security washed over him as he stepped back on the familiar soil of his homeland.

He hailed a cab and gave the address to the driver. The entire time, he stared out the window, seeing the familiar streets in which he once lived in. A smile grazed his lips and he sighed in content.

"You're an American, no?" The driver asked.

Dante turned his head to the driver for a second and noticed how young he looked. He was more or less in his early twenties. Dante wondered what he was doing as a cab driver rather than working.

"Yes. But I have lived here for the first few years of my life." He said, turning back to look at the streets.

"So you have seen how beautiful the land is." Though there was a certain accent in his tone, the driver seemed to speak fluent English.

"Si." Dante didn't want to make conversation. He just wanted to get to his hotel and rest up. He had a long day ahead of him. A meeting with Antonio Valldarri in four hours and a dinner party at his house. One that he did not feel like attending.

"You have business here or on vacation?"

"Business."

"Ah. Our business men here are very," the driver paused, "honorable."

"You seem to know a lot about businessmen." Dante said dryly.

"Si. I drive many around."

Dante looked at him again and saw the proud grin on the driver's face. He saw his chance and took it. "What do you know about Antonio Valldarri?"

The car jolted. Dante's body propelled forward and he grabbed onto the seat in front of him. He cursed. "What the hell?!"

"You're doing business with Mr. Valldarri?" The man looked at Dante with disbelief. "He no do business with Americans."

Dante rolled his eyes and adjusted his suit. "You could have taken it lightly and not try to kill your customers."

"Mi dispiace." The driver started the car again. "Just shocked."

"Is he famous around here?"

The driver nodded. "Si. Very famoso."

Dante muttered a, "Hm."

The car came to a stop. He looked out the window and saw a bellhop standing outside the door. The young man opened it up.

Dante grabbed his luggage and handed it to the bellhop. He placed the money on the awaiting driver's hand and got out of the cab. Straightening up his suit, he walked into the building towards the front desk.

"Dante Hastings." He told the woman at the register. He handed his card to her and leaned against the table.

"Yes, Mr. Hastings. You will be in room 762. Michael will bring everything up for you." The woman handed him back his card along with his pass key. "Have a nice stay."

"Grazi." He muttered. He grabbed the key and walked towards the elevator.

His phone rang just as he got on and he took it without looking at the caller ID. "Dante Hastings."

"Hello, Mr. Hastings. This is Rafael calling from Mr. Valldarri's office. I have called to cancel your appointment with him today. A few issues have come up that requires his attention."

Dante cursed under his breath. The bell dinged and he got off on his floor. He leaned against the wall near the elevator. "Listen, I'm a busy man. Tell him that he meet with me today or no deal."

"You don't understand, Mr. Hastings. This deal is either rescheduled or you can fly back to America."

His voice was starting to give Dante a headache. "Your boss contacted me. He needs me more than I need him."

It was silent on the other end for a few moment before the man spoke up. "Very well. I will inform him of your response."

"Make sure to not waste my time." Dante ended the call and walked towards his room. He opened the door and collapsed on the bed.

This is going to be a long week....Ashley didn't feel anything. She heard and felt nothing. He continued to ramble on to her but she made no response. Her eyes were fogged over but she didn't cry.

"Ashley," he whispered.

She didn't turn to him. Her eyes rested on the windows but she wasn't looking at it. She was motionless. The only sign that she was still alive was the soft breaths that came out every now and then.

"Ashley you have to listen to me." He pleaded.

She clenched her fists and snapped her eyes shut. She allowed her body to collapse on the white lined bed. Her head was turned to the side and a tear slipped down her face.

"Ashley, listen to me. It's crucial that you do." He placed a hand on her shoulder and bent down to be eye level with her.

She looked at him for a few seconds before sliding his hand off of her. She turned over to the other side and buried her eyes into the pillow. "Please. I just want to be alone."

"I know that you're mourning right now but it's very crucial for you to listen to me in this moment. Otherwise, things can get even worse." Desperation was clear in his voice but Ashley didn't want to hear it.

It didn't matter anyways. Not anymore.

"You still have one very healthy fetus left. Please, let me help you keep it that way." He walked over to the other side and hoovered about her again.

"Dr. Carson, please. I just want to be alone."

He sighed. "Alright. I'll come back later to check on you. Your father and brother are waiting outside. I'll inform them and tell them to go home for the day."

Seconds later, he was out the door. His voice came out in hushed whispers as he told her father.

Ashley snapped her eye shut and hugged her pillow tightly. A tear slipped down her face and onto the pillow.

She failed as a mother. ... Samuel punched the wall. Sparks of pain coursed through his knuckles. Red blotches appeared and blood seeped out of his knuckles. A humorless laugh left his mouth. He grabbed his hair and slid down the wall.

He couldn't protect her.

He failed her again.

He should have been there with her. Maybe if he was, something else could have happened differently. He should have been there since the beginning.

But he wasn't.

Maybe if he had protected her better, she wouldn't be going through this pain right now.

A knock came aton his door.

He looked up. His eyes widened. "Mayla?"

Mayla smiled weakly at him. "Hi Samuel. I heard about Ashley and came here as quick as I could. It's good to see you again."

.

.

.

SO CONSTANTINE IS BACCCK GUYS! But will she be as a witch as before? Wait and see.

Love you all of my lovely owlers! <3 <3

Chapter 13

Sorry for the late update guys! Anyways to clear up some stuff

-Mayla is Ashley's best friend and no she is not her mother.

-Constantine is only significant if you read the first version. In this, she's just a random character. So don't worry about her.

-Ashley's step-mother and Samuel's mother is Alessandra.

-Samuel and Ashley do share the same father (not Antonio). Their father is already dead. That backstory will be revealed soon.

-Instead of a sequel, I will do a prequel on Isabella and Antonio. ((:

Anyways, that's it. Enjoy guys. Sorry if it's crap. Rushed it a little bit. Maybe a lot...

.

.

.

Dante chuckled. He leaned over the table and wiped Ashley's mouth with his napkin. He raised his eyebrows up at her and leaned back against his chair. His heart raced in his chest, staring at the beautiful girl who he had the privilege to call his.

"You had some whip cream on your mouth." He said when he saw the questioning look on her face.

A blush made its way to her cheeks.

"Oh." She muttered, looking down at her cup of hot chocolate, shielding her face away from him. She cleared her throat and picked up her cup.

Dante chuckled. He reached his hand over and clutched hers. His fingers brushed over her skin. "Hey don't hide from me." He smiled, picked her hand up and kissed her knuckles.

She smiled at him. Her eyes shined brightly and Dante relished in the fact that he was the reason for that shine. "Do you want to head back to my apartment?" She asked shyly, glancing around the cafe.

Dante nodded his head. He got up and walked over to her side. He pulled her up and kissed her temple. "Let's go."

He took a few couple of bills out of his pocket and placed it on the table. He wrapped his arm around her waist and they walked out of the cafe.

"You know, I don't really know much about your family." Dante muttered, giving her waist a gentle squeeze.

"You know enough." She snapped.

Dante stopped and looked at her.

She sighed. "I'm sorry. I didn't mean to snap at you. It's just, I don't like talking about my family that much. You know that."

Dante resumed walking. He sighed and smiled weakly at her. "I'm sorry. I shouldn't have asked anyways. You're right. You told me enough."

He kissed her temple again.

She smiled gratefully at him and leaned into his side. She wrapped her arms around his waist and kissed his cheek. "I love you Dante."

"I love you too." he muttered back. He clutched her tighter to his body and promised himself to never let go of her.

She is all he needs to survive.

.

.

.

Dante got out of the elevator. He walked over to the receptionist's desk and threw his keys on the counter. He pulled out his credit card and held it up.

The receptionist did not look at him. Rather, he seemed engrossed in whatever was showing on the side. His eyes were wide and there was hint of tears in his eyes.

Dante turned to see what he was staring.

A news report was playing on the T.V.

"Earlier today, Antonia Valldarri's estrange daughter was seen being rushed into the hospital with Valldarri and his stepson in tow. Nothing has been confirmed yet but sources have told us that Valldarri's daughter is currently pregnant and is going through some difficulties with her pregnancy." The woman on the screen said, standing outside a hospital building.

Dante felt his heart drop in his chest.

So that's why Valldarri cancelled the meeting with him.

Or at least, he tried too.

Dante felt like crap.

He should have just rescheduled the meeting. And now that man is probably in so much pain with his daughter,

He sighed and turned back to the receptionist. He waved his credit card in his face.

The boy looked at him and glared, the tears making a bigger appearance. "Put your card away before I shove it up your ass."

He grabbed the keys on the side and rushed out of the building.

Dante's mouth opened in surprise as he looked at the retreating receptionist.

Did that boy just get up in the middle of no where and left? He had a job to do.

Dante huffed in annoyance and tried to keep his cool when the new receptionist came. He nodded at her.

She smiled back at him and went to grab his card when the woman on the T.V. spoke up again.

We have update on the young heiress. According to sources, she had been pregnant with twins. Sadly, one of the twins had died in the womb.

Upon hearing that, Dante thought about Ashley and her babies.

How are they doing? Are they well?

He shook the thought out of his head and glared at the new receptionist. He pushed his card into her face.

She snapped her eyes away from the screen and smiled apologetically at all. "I'm sorry for that sir."

She took the credit card out of his hand and placed the keys next to her mouse.

She slid the card.

"I wonder what you're sorry for." He said sarcastically.

She didn't seem to sense it. "For Frankie storming out earlier. He's our boss's nephew and seeing his cousin in the hospital must hurt him."

Dante raised his eyebrows up at her. "Valldarri owns this hospital?"

The receptionist laughed and handed his card back to him. "He owns all the hotels within a 50 mile radius."

Dante nodded his head in understanding. Whoever was married to Valldarri's daughter was lucky. He would inherit everything.

He looked at the receptionist and tilted his head to the side.

"You seem distressed by the news as well." He remarked, taking his card back.

She shrugged her shoulders. "I went to school with her. We weren't the best of friends but still had each others' back. "

Understanding coursed through him. Dante nodded his head. "Thank you."

He walked out of the hotel and hailed a cab with one thought in his mind.

He had to go apologize to Valldarri and that assistant of his.

.

Valldarri's assistant, Rafael, led him into a room. The boy nodded his head at Dante before turning on his feet and walking out. He closed the door behind him and muttered incoherent words.

Dante sat on one of the chairs in the conference room and pulled out all of his files. He placed them on the table and flipped the file with the contact open. He pulled the contact out and read through it a second time.

Though his eyes skimmed the words on the paper, they didn't register in his mind.

How can it when the only thing he can think about is 'Ashley and her children? The children who wasn't his but yet he still loves.

Why did she have to cheat on him? Was he not good enough for her? Those children made him love them thinking they were his but in the end, they weren't.

He groaned and leaned back against the chair, pulling his hair to the side with his hand. An exasperated sigh left his lips. He leaned back and pulled out his phone. He dialed Thomas's number.

Thomas didn't pick up.

Dante cursed under his breath and pushed his phone back into his pocket.

The door opened.

Dante looked over to it and stood up. He nodded his head at the two men that walked in, both with grim looks on their faces.

They came in front of Dante and shook his hand.

"Good morning. My name is Dante Hastings." Dante greeted.

One of the man, the older one, nodded his head and shook his hand firmly. "Antonio Valldarri." He nudged his briefcase towards the younger man. "This is my son, Samuel."

The younger one didn't say a word. He just shook Dante's hand and sat down across from Dante and next to his father.

"We apologize for our unprofessional behavior earlier. We know that we should not have cancelled but some things came up." The older man said, a look of pain in his eyes.

Dante nodded his head and sat back down. "Let's get started. There's much for us to do." Dante pushed the file towards Antonio and put a pen on top of it. "All you need to do is read it and sign it. After that, we can discuss your business."

Antonio nodded his head. "Very well."

"Your daughter. I heard she was in the hospital." Dante said casually, leaning back against his seat. "It must be hard."

Dante saw the grip of Antonio on the pen tighten. "Yes." He said with pain in his eyes.

"Do you mind if I visit her?" He said. He saw the questioning look on Antonio and Samuel's face and questioned himself the same thing.

Why did he want to visit a stranger?

"Out of respect of course." Dante added in quickly.

Antonio looked over at Samuel and then back at Dante, nodding his head. "Of course. Thank you for caring." He said and signed the papers.

.

Mayla knocked on Ashley's door and then opened it. She smiled softly at Ashley. "Hey." She muttered, walking in. She walked over to the bed and placed the blue roses down on the table. She grabbed a chair and sat down on it. "How are you feeling?"

Ashley shook her head and stared up at the ceiling.

"I just lost my child. How do you think I feel?" She said coldly.

Mayla winced at the ice in her voice. She sighed and brushed a piece of hair away from Ashley's face.

"I'm sorry." She muttered again.

She leaned back against the chair and glanced around the room. She saw a bouquet of white roses on the windowsill and walked over to it. She looked and pulled a card out.

Opening it, she smiled. "You and Samuel made up?"

Mayla looked over at Ashley and saw her nodding her head.

"He's trying to be a better brother." Ashley whispered. A tear slip down her face. "I'm a horrible mother."

Mayla gasped and walked over to Ashley. She grabbed her hand and held it tightly. "Don't say that Ash. It wasn't your fault."

"I couldn't protect her. She was my baby and I couldn't protect her. She died." Ashley's eyes closed as tear after tear slipped down. Her hand moved to her stomach and clutched it. "Look at me Mayla. I'm a pathetic mother."

Mayla felt her own tears coming to the surface. "Don't say that. Everything will be okay again. Just you wait and see. You still have one perfectly healthy baby."

Ashley nodded her head but Mayla knew that nothing would make her feel better at the moment.

How can it? There was no bigger pain than a mother losing her own child.

Mayla knew that better than anyone else.

Mayla stood up and kissed Ashley's forehead. "Get some sleep. I'll be out there if you need me."

She smiled down at Ashley and walked out of the room. She closed the door behind her and leaned against it.

Tears slipped down her face as memories surged forward. She understood better than anyone else how it felt like to lose a child. How helpless one feels when their child is ripped away from them.

She wiped away her tears and turned to the left. Anger coursed into her body. "You!" She shouted. She walked up and slapped him. "What the hell are you doing here?"

"Mayla!" Samuel shouted. "What the hell?"

"Mayla?" He whispered. "What—?"

Mayla slapped him again. "You have no right to be here." She hissed. "Get out."

Dante rubbed his cheek and glared down at her. "I have as much right to be here as you do. This is a public hospital Mayla. Anyone can come here."

Mayla scoffed. Tears slipped down her cheek. "I won't let you come back here and ruin her life. She's already going through so much and don't need you to come back into her life." She whispered.

"Mayla, what's going on?" Samuel muttered, grabbing her hand. He clutched it and looked at her eyes. "Tell me. How do you know Dante?"

"I don't know what you're blabbering about Mayla." Dante said coldly. "She is dead to me. I'm not here for her."

"Then what are you doing with her father and brother you asshole!" Mayla shouted.

Dante's face paled over. "What did you just say?"

"Mayla!" Samuel shouted.

Mayla snapped her head towards Samuel. She pointed towards Dante. "That thing doesn't deserve to be here. He is the reason why Ashley is in that room right now."

Antonio's body froze. "W-what?"

"He's her ex-husband." She hissed.

Chapter 14

C hapter 14

Samuel stared at Ashley's retreating back. His fists clenched and he sat down on the bench, burying his head. He tugged at his hair and wondered what he should do next. She didn't believe him and he expected that.

It still didn't stop the hurt and the clenching of his heart though. He tilted his head up and buried his mouth with both his hands. He had messed up big time. "How do I fix this?" he muttered to himself.

He stood up and shoved his hands into his pockets. He had to find her and try to make her understand. He needs her to forgive him. He can't live with himself until she can.

His sister.

She had been his sister and he treated her like crap all those years before.

He was the reason why she left the estate. Instead of being her biggest protector, he had been her biggest tormentor. He should have been the one who comforted her after a nightmare. Yet he haunted her dreams, taking away her peace of mind.

He could never forgive himself for that.

A tear slipped down his face and he wiped it away hastily. He took another look at the kids. A smile came onto his face when he saw the little girl.

Despite having a cut that would hurt her and hinder her, she still ran around the playground with a big smile on her face. She's strong and Samuel is certain that she could go through anything that life throws at her.

Just like Ashley.

"Excuse me." An angelic voice said.

Samuel turned around. His heart soared inside of his chest, laying eyes on the beauty right in front of him.

A brown haired and blue eyed woman stared back at him. Wearing a pencil skirt and a black blouse, she sported the professional look. Her brown hair had been pinned back and Samuel imagined it down, cascading over her shoulders.

He bit his lip and his eyes wandered down to her chest. He coughed and instantly looked away, praying that she didn't see that he had checked her out.

"Are you Samuel?"

He snapped his head towards her again. Gone is the awkward guy and in his place stood a cautious one. "How did you know my name?"

A scowl came onto her face and she raised her palm up.

Seconds later, Samuel's cheek stung. His hand instinctively raised to his cheek and he glared at the woman. "What the hell?"

"That was for hurting my best friend." She hissed and turned on her heels.

"I don't even know you and you just slapped me?" Samuel shouted. He walked forward and grabbed her wrist, turning her around. "Apologize."

She freed her wrist and glared at him. "The name is Mayla Reilly. It'll be best if you remember the name. After all, this would not be the last time that you hear about me."

With that being said, she turned around and left him.

Samuel's mouth dropped open. He stared at the infuriating woman walking away.

She went up to him and slapped him for no reason at all, claiming to have done it on her best friend's behalf. Who was the best friend that got that girl so riled up for her to punch him?

Was it someone that he slept with and dropped?

Samuel cringed at the thought of his immature ways years back. If he could turn back the clock, he would change so many things about himself, first starting with how he treated Ashley. But he can't. So now all he can do, is try to make himself become a better man.

A man in which his future kids can look up to and be proud that he's their father.

But for now, he must make sure that he becomes that man.

.

.

He's her ex-husband.

The words continued to echo throughout Samuel's mind. He looked at Dante and felt anger coursing through his veins. He's the reason that Ashley is in that hospital room. The reason why Ashley is heartbroken beyond compare.

Samuel only saw red.

He didn't think before he raised his fist and pounded it against Dante's nose.

Pain pierced through his knuckles but he ignored it and shook it off. He pushed Antonio to the side and walked forward. Grabbing Dante by his collar, he pushed him against the wall. "So you're the reason why Ashley is in pain right now?"

Satisfaction coursed inside of him as Dante coughed. One hand held Samuel's wrist while the other clutched his bleeding nose.

"Let me go." Dante coughed.

Samuel glared at Dante and threw him to the side. "Can't even defend yourself? You're pathetic."

Samuel felt a comforting hand on his shoulder, stopping him from kneeling down next to Dante to land another blow.

He didn't need to look to know that it was Mayla. His anger start diminished for a second. But all it took was one glance at Dante for his anger to surged through again.

"What the hell did you punch me for? I didn't do anything to you." Dante glared at him.

"You didn't do anything to me but you sure as hell did something to piss me off." Samuel took a step forward.

Mayla placed a hand on his chest, stopping him.

He turned to her and stared into her eyes. "What?" He shouted at her.

Mayla glared at him.

Samuel cleared his throat, loosening the tie around his neck.

"Stop. He's not worth you being thrown out of the hospital." Mayla said coldly making Samuel wince.

He shook his head.

Now is not to time to get offended at all how Mayla talks to him.

"He hurt Ashley." Samuel turned back to Dante and glared at him. "Get out of here before I do worse."

"Not until you explain to me what's going on and why you punched me." Dante wiped the blood that dripped down his face.

Samuel chuckled and walked forward. "Do you want to land a spot here as a patient?"

"We don't need to explain anything to you. Leave before," Mayla paused, "before we both do something we regret."

Samuel clenched his fist. "I regret not asking who her husband was. If I did, I would have punched him before signing that contract. He's the reason why the only woman I give a crap about is in paint. Ashley deserves better than him and I will make sure she finds better."

Dante stared at him for five seconds. He turned towards Mayla, his gaze softening. "Ashley. She's the one that's in there?"

Mayla stayed silent.

"Why does it matter to you? You cut off all ties with her already." Samuel crossed his arms over his chest.

Dante glared at Samuel. "I don't know who you are to Ashley but I have a pretty good guess."

Samuel chuckled humorlessly. "I can already tell what you're going to say."

He walked forward, staring down at Dante.

Dante glared at him and pushed him back.

Samuel rolled his eyes. "You think I'm her lover don't you. You think I'm the father to her babies because how protective I am towards her. You think I'm the reason behind your divorce."

"How—"

"I see how you looked at me. Like I was a challenge. But maybe if you had listened to Mayla you would have heard. I'm her brother. Want to know something else? No one ruined your marriage but you. Ashley didn't do shit and neither did I. It was all you and your stupid paranoia. Ashley told me all about those pictures you got that made her seem like a cheater. She showed me copies of them. You're a lawyer. You should have known better. They were all photoshopped but you were too blind to fucking see it. Because of your stupidity, you let the best girl slip through your fingertips. Now, you lost her forever. You're never going to be able to win her back, no matter how hard you try." Samuel shook his head. "I won't let that happen. I'll be dead before I even let her call you a friend."

Dante took a step back.

Realization and then pain flashed through his eyes and he turned to the hospital door. He shook his head and his face became emotionless again. "I wouldn't even dream of chasing after her again."

He gave Antonio a quick nod before turning his back and walking away.

"He was her ex-husband? Dante Hastings is the man that hurt my little girl?" Antonio whispered, speaking up for the first time.

Samuel looked at Mayla.

She nodded her head at them and then looked towards Ashley's room.

"We can't let her know." she whispered, "it will only stress her out more."

Samuel didn't say anything.

He walked towards Ashley's room and opened the door. He slammed it shut behind him.

Ashley jumped and turned to him.

Samuel smiled weakly. "Sorry. I didn't mean to startle you." He said, walking over to her bedside. He brushed his hand across her hair. "How are you feeling?"

Ashley gave him a weak smile. "Better than before."

Samuel looked at her with worry. "Don't lie to me, Ash. I may not have been there for you but I'm your brother. I know when you're lying."

That all it took for Ashley to burst into tears.

Samuel pulled her into a hug. He wrapped his arms around her frail body, letting her soak her tears into his blazer.

"Sh. It's okay baby girl. I'm here. I'm not going to go anywhere. I'm going to stay right here with you. We'll get through this." he whispered, kissing her forehead. He closed his eyes.

A tear slipped down his face, knowing that there's nothing he can really do to ease her. He couldn't do anything to make her feel better about herself.

Once again, he felt like a useless brother.

.

.

.

Mayla sat down on the hospital chair and leaned her head against the wall. She closed her eyes and her knuckles formed into a fist.

She felt pathetic.

She shouldn't have stopped Samuel from beating Dante into a pulp. She should have allowed Dante to be hurt.

Be hurt like how he had hurt her best friend.

But a part of her knew that Ashley wouldn't have want Samuel or her to have done that.

Ashley hated violence and didn't believe that there is any reason for revenge.

That was just the type of person Ashley was.

She was too forgiving even to those that didn't deserve it. She couldn't see that those people would only just continue to hurt her.

People like Dante.

Mayla prayed that Ashley wouldn't forgive Dante and let him back into her life.

She deserved better than Dante and she hoped that Ashley would realize that. Ashley deserved a man who respected her and would not jump to conclusions. One who would consult her about their problems rather than dropping her the moment one arises.

"What are you thinking about?"

Mayla opened her eyes and turned to the side. She smiled and shrugged her shoulders. "About how messed up everything is right now."

He chuckled but there was no humor in his voice. He sat down next to her and leaned his head back. "Do you remember the first time we met?"

Mayla nodded her head, a smile coming to her face. "I slapped you."

He laughed, a genuine one this time. One that sent Mayla's heart into overdrive.

"I was so confused. There I was, minding my own business and this little spitfire comes up to me and slaps me for no apparent reason." He said, looking at Mayla.

Mayla looked back at him, getting lost in his eyes. She leaned forward for a second but quickly realizing what had happened. She moved back. She nudged his side. "Hey, this spitfire is no where near little."

"I know. I saw everything there is to her before." Samuel said with a smirk.

Mayla gasped and slapped his chest. She turned to the side, hearing his chuckle. Her cheeks must now resemble that of a tomato.

She's falling.

And she's falling hard.

.

.

.

Hi you guys! Sorry this one took so long. I know I know. Yalls must hate me :((I have good news for you guys though. I have two months left of school so that means...TWO MORE MONTHS UNTIL I START UPDATING REGULARLY! YAY AMIRITE?

Okay so with that being said, I really hope you guys enjoyed that chapter. Do I sense a little something something going on between Mayla and Samuel? Olala. Do you ship or nawh? ;)

Anyways, I guess I'll see you guys next time!

Love you all of my lovely owlers!

~Amber <3 <3 <3

Chapter 15

This is a short chapter but don't you worry my lovelies. I have the next one coming up soon ;)

Enjoy.

.

.

.

Chapter 15

I could still feel his touch on my skin.

The way his rough hand left behind scratches as he trails his hand up and down my arm.

I wanted to push him away and jump into a pool of water to wash away the sins of his hand. I didn't want him to touch me. Not like that. All I could feel in the bile rising in my throat as he continued his assault on my body.

I remember it so clearly.

How his breath burned my neck, sending a feeling of desperation down my body. Desperation to get away from him and into the arms of who would always protect me no matter what.

But I had been frozen in place. The only thing that showed any reaction was the tear that slipped down my cheek.

He tugged my shirt down and whispered in my ear. "No one can ever replace what we have. You are mine and I am yours."

I remembered how I beg him. I remembered the exact words. "Please don't do this to me. I beg you. Let me go."

A force slammed itself into my body and I found myself hitting the cold ground. I looked up, the tears falling down faster than before.

"Don't you ever beg me to let you go. You are mine."

He took off his clothes and that was the end of it.

He kept me with him until he felt like it was safe enough to let me go. He got what he wanted from me.

He made me feel disgust in myself. He made me detest the touch of any man on my body. He ruined my body, mind, and soul.

They told me that I will get better. Everyone tells me the same thing. Everyone has the same pitiful look in their eyes when they looked at me. Everyone kept reassuring me that everything will be okay.

But I know, nothing will be okay anymore.

~Isabella Valldarri.

.

.

.

I stared at the blank white wall, feeling the familiar feeling of emptiness inside of me.

The feeling that made its home in my mind, refusing to ever leave me. Taking over my life with it's blank thoughts and expressions, I continue to sit day in and out, never leaving the confines of this room.

My husband does not hold me anymore. He, like I, could not bare the sight of my own skin. The skin that has been tarnished by the man who took every single ounce of happiness away from me. Antonio can't even look at me without crying.

I wanted to cry along with him. I wanted to mourn the loss of our lives but I couldn't. No matter how much I try to feel, I couldn't.

I know he blames himself for not protecting me. I see the look in his eyes.

He looks defeated.

Just like I was.

~Isabella Valldarri

.

.

.

He's in jail now. After three weeks of searching for him, they caught him. He didn't try to put up a fight. The day where I decided to leave my sanctuary is the day I see Lorenzo surrendering himself to the officers. He gave me a message though.

I know he saw me. I had seen the smile on his face as he looked towards my direction. A smile that brought me back to when he had stripped me of who I am. A smile that promised me that he would return and reclaim me again.

A smile that finally brought one feeling back into my body.

Fear.

~Isabella Valldarri

.

.

.

Lorenzo had gifted me something from my imprisonment. Something that I never knew he had given me.

He had given me a child.

~Isabella Valldarri

.

.

.

"You know now, don't you?"

Ashley looked up and hugged her mother's journal closer to her chest. She wiped away the tears that fell down her cheeks. "That's why you hated me, didn't you?" she whispered, looking into her eyes.

Alessandra nodded her head. "My husband left me just so he could force himself on a woman who wouldn't even give him a second look."

"I'm the result of that night," Ashley whispered. "Antonio, he raised me knowing I was the daughter of the man who raped his wife."

Alessandra closed her eyes. "I blamed your mother when I should have blamed myself instead."

"What did you do?" Ashley whispered.

She closed her eyes and for the first time, Ashley saw a trace of vulnerability in the woman. "It doesn't matter anymore." She opened her eyes and gone was the vulnerable woman.

Back in its stead is the woman who destroyed Ashley's life.

She cracked a smile and tilted her head to the side. "Well, you seem well now."

Ashley didn't move or say anything. She continued to stare at Alessandra, wondering what had led this woman to become so cold and evil. A part of her felt pity towards Alessandra.

The woman didn't seem to have anything but wealth but what was the wealth if she didn't have a family to share it with.

"You know, Samuel changed. He defied my orders just to protect you. Protect the girl he hated ever since he was a little boy." Alessandra walked closer to her and laughed humorlessly.

Ashley's finger itched out to the button at the side of her bed. She touched it softly, ready to press on it if Alessandra gives her a reason to.

Alessandra seemed to have noticed as she stopped and smirked.

"Ashley, dear, do you not trust me? Why darling, I am hurt." The woman mocked, putting her hand over her chest.

Ashley only stared at her.

Alessanda laughed and turned around. "You're weak just like your mother had been, Ashley. You constantly pity yourself instead of sucking it up and being a woman. Maybe that's why you lost one of the twins."

Ashley's eyes widened and a tear slipped down.

Alessandra's fist clenched. "You know I'm right, don't you." She laughed but there was no denying the pain in the sound. "Someone had to be the one to tell you this."

"Alessandra," Ashley whispered.

She turned her head to Ashley and gave her a hard look. "You're not getting anywhere by being a softie, Ashley. People are going to continue to take advantage of you until you start to take control of your own life." She turned back around and walked out of the door, leaving a cold aura behind her.

.

.

.

A knock came at her door. She pulled herself up from her bed. "Come in."

A man stepped through the door, holding a clipboard. He looked up at her with an emotionless expression on his face. "You must be Ashley. My name is Dr. Morcelli. How are you feeling today?"

Ashley looked at him. "What happened to Dr. Carson?"

"He's away right now. I'll be in charge of you until you are dismissed." He had an empowering voice that demands the attention from those he was talking to. He would have made a good businessman if he hadn't chosen to become a doctor.

Ashley's stomach swirled. She placed her hand on it and saw Dr. Morcelli glancing down at her stomach. "I feel alright." She muttered.

"That doesn't help me." He grumbled. He pulled out his stethoscope and walked over to her side. He pressed it down on her chest.

Ashley turned away from him and stared out the window.

After a few seconds, he pulled it away and nodded his head, jotting down notes on his clipboard. "Alright your heartbeat seems stable. I would suggest staying here for an extra day for me to check up on you but it's all on you now."

Ashley nodded her head. She needed to do what was best for her remaining child. "I'll stay for another day."

It had been quick but Dr. Morcelli's lips tilted before it was placed in a fine line again. "Good. I'll be back around noon to check up on you again. Try not to get stressed."

"Of course."

"Also you might want to pull up your gown a bit." His voice had been stern but the quick look of amusement in his eyes betrayed him.

Ashley looked down and blushed when she saw part of her bra showing.

The gown had slipped down a decent enough amount for Dr. Morcelli to see how gifted she is.

She hastily pulled it up and looked at the clock on top of his head. "T-thanks." she muttered.

"Di niente." He said, leaving.

Ashley let out a sigh. She laid back on her bed and placed her hand over her stomach.

"Please, don't leave me." She whispered.

She clutched her stomach protectively and closed her eyes to sleep.

She didn't have them closed for five minutes before she heard the door opening again. Groaning at how her sleep keeps getting interrupted, she opened her eyes and stared at the door.

Her body froze and her heart beat faster in her chest. Her fists clenched itself around the bed sheets and her eyes narrowed into slits.

"Dante." His name burned on her tongue and her body scooted back further into the bed, wanting to be away from him.

Dante shoved his hand into his pocket and gave her the smile that she used to love some much. "Hello Ashley."

.

.

.

Is it just me or does Dr. Morcelli sound like super hot? Hm...I wonder how big his role is going to be ;)

AND OMFG GUYS! DANTE IS IN ASHLEY'S HOLY CRAPPUCCI-NO.

UNTIL NEXT TIME MY LOVELIES!

Love you all of my lovely owlers!!!

~Amber <3 <3 <3

Chapter 16

T old you I'd have it out soon. ;)

Enjoy it my lovelies!

.

.

.

Chapter 16

"Ashley come on. Don't be mad about this." Dante said, putting his hand on her shoulders. "I swear, I didn't know she was going to do that."

Ashley shrugged his hand off and turned around.

Dante sighed, "Now will you just let me exp-"

She slapped him across his face. "How dare say that to me? You pulled away from her, smiled, and resumed your little show?" She clenched her fist and shook her head, chuckling emotionlessly. "How stupid do you think I am?"

Dante held his cheek and glared at her. "Will you just listen to me for once? Let me explain myself."

She chuckled again and sat down on her couch. "I heard them talking in class today. She told me how you came to her apartment last night, asking for it."

He shook his head violently. He walked over to her and grabbed her wrist. "I didn't do that. You should know I wouldn't do anything to hurt you."

She tried to pull her arm back but he held on tighter. She winced as his grip continued to tighten on her arm. "You're hurting me right now."

"Just listen to me then." He released her arm.

"Listen to you about what? Dante we've only been dating for a month." She said, glaring at him. "One month and you already messed up."

"You lasted longer than any girl ever. That means something, Ashley." Dante reassured. He kneeled on the ground and placed his hand on her knees.

She scoffed and pushed his hand away. She felt fear course in her when she saw how irritated he got but covered it up. "That's how you're going to defend yourself?" She laughed. "Wow. I feel so special."

Dante groaned and brushed his hand through his hair. "Please. Just let me explain." he begged her.

She crossed her arms over her chest and leaned back against the couch. "Enlighten me with your story."

He inhaled. "Listen, she grabbed me and kissed me. It had been dark and I thought she was you. I mean, she kissed like you—"

"That's not an excuse."

He sighed and nodded his head. "I know but I had too much to drink. I wasn't thinking straight." He looked up at her. "Do you forgive me?"

She sighed and grabbed his hand. "Can you just give me time right now. I don't know." With that she released his hand and looked to the side.

He sighed and seconds later, the door closed.

She released a breath that she didn't know she was holding and got up from the couch. She walked over to her window and saw him walking down the stairs.

Her heart tugged in her chest.

It seemed unreal at what had happened.

She didn't know what to think about them anymore.

It doesn't seem like Dante's ready to give up his lifestyle. He seemed like he isn't as committed as he claimed he was.

.

.

.

"What are you doing here?" She moved her finger to the button on the side of her bed. "Why are you in Italy?"

He shrugged his shoulders and motioned to the chair next to her bed. "May I?" He asked, taking off his blazer. He placed in the crook of his arm and smiled at her.

"No." She said.

He chuckled although there had been nothing funny about her comment. "You seem to never lose that sass of yours." He said dryly, before sitting himself on the chair. He leaned back against it and stared at her. "How are you?"

"What you you doing here?" She asked again, ignoring his question. She scoffed and then smiled dryly at him. "Finally realized your mistake?"

"I made no mistake at all. I didn't do anything wrong, you did. But I'm not here to talk about that." He looked around her room. "You haven't seem to be taking care of yourself." He turned back to her and smirked. "Why? Did you missed me too much?"

"Not onc bit." She laughed humorlessly. "I honestly thought I would but I stopped caring. I realized I stopped caring for you the moment I realized that life isn't always filled with rainbows and butterflies."

He chuckled again. "That's one thing I didn't miss about you. Your attitude."

Anger coursing through her veins. Anger that didn't seem to be there before until he waltzed into her room.

He knew nothing about her.

He knew nothing about what she had been going through.

Her heart beat in her chest and she gripped the side of her bed. "I won't ask you a fourth time. What are you doing here? If you can't answer that, then leave." She said, clenching her teeth.

He frowned at her. "Fine." He stood up and faced his face directly in front of hers. "Why didn't you tell me your father had been Antonio Valldarri?"

Ashley moved back against her bed and stared at the chair where he had been sitting. "Why does that matter to you?"

Dante punched the wall above her head.

Ashley jumped and instantly grabbed onto her stomach, shielding it. "What the hell, Dante?" She shouted. She got off the bed and walked to the other side.

"I would have loved to know that my client had been the father of my wife." He shouted, walking towards her with a menace in his steps.

Ashley froze. Her hand released her stomach and laid limp at her side. "Y-you're my father's new client."

Dante laughed and leaned against the wall. "Funny how fate works doesn't it? I get to be the lawyer of the man who fathered my whore of a wife."

The word didn't seem to pierce her heart like she thought it would. She thought it would cause her pain, hearing that word coming from him but didn't. It didn't hurt one bit. It only caused her to laugh at him.

"Whore? You're calling me the whore?" She stopped laughing and glared at him. "Why don't you look in the mirror?"

Dante glared at her and got off the wall. He walked towards her with his fists clenched, his knuckles turning white.

He's getting angry. And if there's one thing that Ashley knew about Dante is that when he gets angry, he would do things that he normally wouldn't do. His anger got the best of him and she had been on the receiving end once or twice before.

Fearing for her daughter's life, Ashley moved closer to the door and froze when a hand placed itself on her shoulder. She turned around and saw Dr. Morcelli.

He didn't look at her. His stare was tight on Dante.

She looked closer into his eyes and saw fury burning in them. "Dr. Morcelli." She whispered.

He moved her gently behind him. "Who are you?" He directed the question towards Dante. He shoved his hands into the pockets of his coat.

"It doesn't matter who I am. Leave. My wife and I have some business to talk about." Dante said, glaring at Dr. Morcelli.

"Ex-wife. We had a divorce. A divorce that you wanted! And now you're back here claiming—" Ashley curled up and clenched her stomach. She closed her eyes and prayed. God no. Please no.

She felt hands placed on her shoulders and opened her eyes. Dr. Morcelli's bright blue eyes glanced back at her, worry swimming in them. "Are you okay?"

"It hurts." She whispered.

He guided her back to her bed and helped her lay down it. Both of them ignored Dante and focused on her stomach.

"I need to raise your gown, that okay?" he looked at her for her permission.

She nodded.

He sighed in relief and pulled her gown up until it revealed her stomach.

"What's going on right now?" Dante asked. And for the first time in forever, Ashley heard worry in his voice.

"Dawn!" Dr. Morcelli shouted. He put his hands on top of Ashley's stomach and pressed against it gently.

Ashley winced and closed her eyes. "What's happening to my baby?" She whispered. She clenched her hand on the bed sheets.

Dr. Morcelli didn't answer but continued to press gentle touches to her stomach.

She opened her eyes and looked at him. "Answer me please. What's happening?"

"What is it, Alessio?" A woman asked, coming into the room.

"Have security escort the man out. He's causing distress for the patient which is not good for her or her child." He responded, looking at the woman for a second before turning back to Ashley. He pressed down on her lower stomach again. "Does that hurt?"

Ashley bit down on her lip and nodded her head. "Yes."

"Sir, please follow me." The woman spoke up again.

"I'm not going anywhere." Dante said.

"Sir, I won't ask you again. Please come with me." The woman asked again but this time, her voice held a threat to it.

"I have the right to know what's going on with her. She's my wife."

"Ex-wife." Ashley corrected again while wincing.

She opened her eyes and glared at Dante. "Leave my room. I don't want to see you in here."

He glared back at her and clenched his fist. "I have to talk to you still."

"I don't care about what you have to say. We got our divorce already just like you wanted. What more do you want from me?" Ashley shouted, sitting up a bit but laid back down when Morcelli's hand pushed her gently back on the bed.

"Calma." He ordered her. "Dawn, get security."

"Already did." the woman replied.

"I want the f*cking truth from you!" Dante shouted, pushing the woman away when she came closer to him.

"What truth?!" Ashley shouted back.

"Ashley you have to stay calm."

"Why did you cheat on me? I want to know that," He glared at her, his chest moving up and down at a rapid pace. "We were happy."

"I never cheated on you at all." she hissed out. "It had been all you. Through all the times that you messed up, I forgave you. I had always been mad but I always listened to your explanations."

Dante stared at her, his hands forming fists at his side.

"I never cheated on you but you never allowed me the chance to give you an explanation," she whispered.

Dante opened his mouth but Ashley continued on.

"You continued to assume and make me the bad guy when it was you. I always forgave you because I loved you.I see how stupid I had been for all the things I gave up for you. My job, my life, and my heart but you couldn't do the same."

Dante glared at her. "You cheated on me."

Ashley glared at him and sat up only to be pushed down gently by Dr. Morcelli. "I never cheated on you!" she screamed at him. Her eyes rolled back in her head and she closed her eyes.

"That's it." Morcelli explained. He removed his hand and grabbed Dante who started to resist him. "You need to get out. A fucker like you will only cause more harm." He pushed Dante out of the door as if he was just a plastic bag.

The woman got out of the room and had security drag Dante away.

Ashley opened her eyes.

"Are you okay?"

Panting heavily, Ashley took one look at Dr. Morcelli and bursted into tears. She grabbed a hold of her stomach again and held onto it. Pain continued to erupt all around her and she prayed for the pain to end soon.

"Cazzo. Ashley breathe. You need to breathe right now."

Ashley felt him hovering over her head and a buzzer let her know that he had called for backup. She closed her eyes and clenched her stomach tighter. "It hurts! Please help me." she begged him, tears running down her face.

The door slammed open and a rush of people came in it.

"She's not calming down. Someone give me a sedative!" His voice echoed through the room, ringing louder than ever before.

She felt a sting on her arm before she laid back on the bed. She looked at Dr. Morcelli who had worry plastered all over his face. "Save her. Save my daughter." she whispered before succumbing to the darkness.

.

.

.

Um...I take it that I must hide now?

OKAY BYE GUYS! UMM! YOU'LL NEVER CATCH ME ALIVE!

Love you all of my lovely owlers!

~Amber <3 <3 <3

Chapter 17

Wowza! Another chapter after only a day? Three chapters in a week?! what?! Don't get too used to it guys. I can feel my teachers piling up my homework as we speak. Anyways, hope you guys enjoy this chapter!

.

.

.

Chapter 17

Dante looked over at his girlfriend, his eyes lighting up at the sight of her. He looked back onto the road and smiled to himself.

Girlfriend.

When was the last time that he had one of that? Probably in middle school. Girls were never special to him. It had all been fun and games.

All until he met her.

She captivated him ever since the first time her saw her. With her wavy brown hair and her deep brown eyes, she stole all of his attention.

He never looked at a girl the same way that he has looked at her.

She is his everything.

He reached his right hand out and intertwined his fingers with hers. He looked at her, seeing her beautiful smile gracing her face. He smiled back at her and ran his thumb on her skin, turning his attention back to the road again.

"I'm scared?" she whispered.

"Of what?" Dante stole a quick glance, seeing the cute worried look on her face. He chuckled. That is a face that he has gone accustomed to seeing every single day since their first date together.

"Well, I am meeting your mother for the first time ever. That's a little nerve-wracking." she responded.

He chuckled and turned on the street. He pulled up into the house and placed the car in park. He looked over at her, leaned over, and kissed her forehead. He held her hand up and kissed her knuckles.

Ashley looked at him with a smile on her face.

"My mom is going to love you. You're the first girl I ever introduced as my girlfriend," he said pressing another kiss on her knuckles.

He grinned when he saw the teasing smile gaze Ashley's lips. "That's because you've been busy being a manwhore."

He rolled his eyes and grinned at her. "Well, that all changed since the moment I started dating you, didn't it?"

"Yet girls still throw themselves at you." She tried to make it sound like a joke but Dante knew how much it bothered her when he talked to other girls.

They had constant misunderstandings that had to always be cleared up. It had always bothered him how little she trusted him but he knew a girl like her had a hard time trusting guys like him. Afterall, her father had kicked her out without a perfect explanation.

"You know they don't mean anything." he caressed her face and smiled lovingly at her. "You're the only girl that matters."

She shoved his shoulders and nudged her head to the house. "What about the woman who birthed you?"

"My mother could never compare to anyone." he grinned, staring at the house. "She's just the best there is."

Ashley laughed, the sound bringing joy into Dante's heart. "You're such a mama's boy. Hard to imagine with that macho image that you carry."

"Underneath all this muscle, there is just a small boy who wants a hug from his mother." Dante smiled and opened his door. He quickly jogged over to the other side and opened up Ashley's door also. He bowed. "Milady."

Ashley laughed and shoved him out of the way. She got out of the car and placed her hand into his awaiting ones. She took a deep breath. "Are you sure your mother is going to like me? I don't know what to do if she doesn't."

"She's not going to like you." Dante said seriously.

Ashley gasp and reached for the car handle. "Okay, i'm going home then."

Dante laughed and pulled her into his chest. He stared down into her eyes. "She's going to love you." he whispered. He leaned down and pecked her lips softly.

"Now, don't start making babies on my front lawn."

Dante grinned and pulled away from Ashley. He released her hand and ran over to the front door. He engulfed his mother into a hug, spinning her around. "I missed you mom."

His mother laughed and patted his shoulders. "Okay Dante. You can let me down now."

He placed her back down at the ground. Turning around, he smiled at Ashley and signaled her to come forward. As Ashley came closer, he pulled her into his arms. He looked at his mother and grinned. "Mom, this is my girlfriend, Ashley."

His mother's eyes widened and she looked from Dante to Ashley. "Girlfriend?! Since when?!"

Ashley looked at her nervously and pulled a piece of hair behind her ear. "Hello, Ms. Hastings. My name is—"

"Oh I want nothing of that." His mother grinned and pulled Ashley into an unexpected hug. "Call me Violet."

Ashley looked shocked and Dante sniggered at her expression. She slowly wrapped her arms around his mother.

"Oh, finally. You bought home a decent girl for me." His mother exclaimed happily, pulling away from Ashley. She wiped away an imaginary tear. "I could die a happy woman now."

Dante laughed at her theatrics. "Mother."

His mother looked at him and glared. "What? Let your mother be happy. You always bought home tramps and finally brought home a nice looking girl." She turned to Ashley. "Come on in dear, I'll bake you a pie." With that, she walked into the house, humming a happy tune.

Dante turned to Ashley and laughed. "Told you that she'd love you."

Ashley smiled and pecked his lips. "I already love her also."

.

.

.

Dante got out of the hospital building, rage building inside of him. He stood to the side and with a scream, he punched the wall. Agony flowed through his nerves but it had been nothing next to the agony raging inside of his heart.

He looked up at the building and glared at it. He couldn't believe what had just happened. They had kicked him out of the hospital all together, putting his name down on the reject list. Did they not know who he was and how fast he can ruin them?

His mind drifted off to her. To Ashley.

He couldn't help but let the worry seep into his body. The worry of whether or not she'll be okay.

The last look that he got of her showed her in immense pain.

He didn't want to admit it but he knew that pain had been caused by him. He should have been happy that she felt pain but all he felt was worry and heartbreak.

A part of him still wanted to continue to believe that she had never cheated but the encrypting photos said otherwise.

It had been ironic how things had turned out.

She constantly accused him of cheating yet she had no evidence but she had been the cheater all along. And he had the evidence to prove it.

She doubted him when all along, it should have been him doubting her. He loved her with every ounce of his beating heart but she couldn't return his feelings. If she had loved him, she wouldn't have cheated.

But then he remembered Samuel's words and he felt his world crashing all around him all over again.

What Samuel said.

It couldn't be true right?

He's a lawyer, of course he's going to know if a photo is photoshopped or not. That photo seemed all the way real.

But should he take the chance?

He pulled out his phone and called Thomas.

"Hey, how's Italy." Thomas answered within the third ring.

"The pictures of Ashley. Run them through for me. Figure out if they were photoshopped or not." he demanded, getting straight to the point.

"Well hello to you too." Thomas muttered. Dante heard some ruffling on his end. "Alright I'll do that right now."

"Okay."

"Dante?" Thomas's voice held curiosity.

"What is it?" Dante asked with a hint of roughness.

"What got you to finally see that you should have gotten it check? You never wanted to before. Why start now?"

Dante sighed and pinched the bridge of his nose. "I need to know the truth, to decide whether or not I should—"

"I understand." He paused for a second. "Listen, you can't forget about the deal with Valldarri. Remember what I said about the daughter. She's your gate-way right now. He doesn't have a son. He might give us some of the shares. We need this deal, Dante."

Dante looked up at the building, specifically the floor that Ashley is in. For the first time, he grinned. "Don't worry. That deal is as good as ours. I got him the sign the first part already."

"Alright, don't mess this one up."

"I won't." he promised.

.

.

.

Mayla ran straight into the hospital building, ignoring the familiar figure standing right outside it, talking on the phone. She fast walked towards the receptionist. "Ashley Valldarri. Had she been moved?"

The receptionist nodded her head and hand Mayla a pass. "You need that to get into ICU."

Mayla's face paled over. "The ICU? What happened to her?"

The receptionist shrugged her shoulders and looked at Mayla in pity. "Dr. Morcelli will explain to you when you get there."

Mayla nodded her head. She thanked her before running straight into the elevator. She quickly pressed on the floor she needed to be on and closed the doors. The music in the elevator did nothing ease her worries.

The passing seconds caused her to think about the worst case scenarios.

When the door finally opened, Mayla booked it out of there. She ran to a near-by nurse. "I need to see Dr. Morcelli."

The nursed opened her mouth but then closed it. She pointed her finger behind Mayla.

Mayla turned around and saw a handsome looking doctor looking at her with his hands shoved into the pockets of his scrubs. He motioned for her to follow him. She walked into his office and sat down on one of the chairs.

"Please, can you tell me what happened with Ashley?"

He pulled out a file and looked at her. "Are you her family member?"

"I'm her brother's wife." she lied.

He raised his eyebrows up at her. "Only immediate family members can make a decision regarding Ashley's health. Are you sure that you're her brother's wife?"

She nodded her head. "Yes."

He nodded his head though he didn't seem to believe her. He opened up the file. "It seems as though you're the first person Ashley had put down to make any health related decisions if she were unable to."

Worry coursed through Mayla. "Is it that bad that she can't make her own decisions?" she whispered.

Alessio nodded. "She's under a sedative now but we need a decision made now."

"What's wrong with her?" Mayla whispered.

Alessio sighed. "Ashley suffered from HELLP syndrome."

Mayla furrowed her eyebrows at him. "What does that mean?"

"She has a combined liver and blood clotting problem." he explained. He put the file down and crossed his arms. "The only way to treat this condition is to deliver the baby."

Mayla's eyes widened. "Now?"

He nodded his head.

Mayla shook hers, tears coming into her eyes. "You can't. The baby. It's not going to make it at this early stage."

"She's in a very critical stage right now. If we don't deliver the baby," he gulped, "she might not be able to make it."

"No. You will save the baby." Mayla stated firmly.

He looked at her in shocked. "Listen the baby has a low chance of making it whether or not we deliver now or in two more months. It's better that we save the mother."

Mayla shook her head. She stood up. "I know her. She would want to do what is best for her child. You may have her best interest at heart but I have her best wishes. She will never be able to live knowing that her baby had a chance of survival but wasn't able to get it."

"Is that the decision that you will go with?" he asked her coldly. "There is a 70% chance that she won't even make it and a 60% chance that the baby wouldn't either."

Mayla closed her eyes and prayed that she made the right decision. "Yes." she whispered.

"Alright then. There's still time for you to change your mind." He nodded at her and walked out of the door.

Mayla felt a tear slip down her face at the thought of losing her best friend. But she knew deep inside of her heart that she had made the right decision.

This is what Ashley would want.

.

.

.

Alessio Morcelli walked towards her hospital room. He opened the door and walked in. His eyes zoomed in on the heart monitor beating at its normal rate. He sighed and looked at her charts. Everything seemed to be good so far.

His eyes zoomed in on her stomach and he placed a gentle hand on it. He felt a small kick and a sense of protectiveness came over him.

"Dr. Morcelli." she whispered hoarsely.

He removed his hand and helped her up the bed. He held up a glass of water to her lips and helped her. "How are you feeling?"

She nodded her head. Her hands went to her stomach. "Better." she muttered.

He nodded his head. "Ashley, I need you to answer me honestly."

She looked at him with confusion. "What is it?"

"Do you love your child?"

She gasped and nodded her head. "Of course I do. What kind of question is that? My baby is everything to me right now."

He gave her a solemn look. "Would you risk your own life for you child?"

"In a heartbeat." she responded without a moment of hesitation.

He nodded his head and for the first time, smiled at her. "Feel better soon. I'll be back to check on you in an hour. Rest up."

He walked out of the door before she could say anything. Shoving his hands into his pockets, he closed his eyes. A sigh left his lips.

He knew what he needed to do.

.

.

.

I just keep making you guys hate me more and more don't I? Oh wells.

Love you all of my lovely owlers!

~Amber <3 <3 <3

Chapter 18

You guys can thank a fellow owler for this. Her message brought a thousand of tears rushing down my face seeing the impact that I made on her life. Writing is a powerful tool you guys. All kinds of writing is beautiful because it expresses the mind of a person. You could never know it but everything you say, do, express, write, can change a person's life and might even end up saving them. So I implore all of you to write. Write your feelings away. Write poems, short stories, songs, epics, anything your heart desires. You are all readers but why don't you all become writers also. And if you do happen to share your work, do not let other people's discouragement bring you down. Allow that to be your motivation to keep writing. All writers will get discouragement from others. No one is bad at writing. You're only as bad as you make yourself to be. Write for yourself.

And guys, don't be scared to message me. I love getting messages from you guys. It might take me some time to reply but I do try to reply to all. ((:

With that being said, I hope you guys enjoy this chapter. <3

Chapter 18

Antonio and I have discussed about the child. We'll keep him or her. Antonio will be the only father that they'll ever know. The name Lorenzo will never be spoken of inside this house once the child is born.

Through everything, Antonio have been very helpful towards me.

He made sure I had been comfortable at all times. He treated this child as if he or she is his own. His love for me never seemed to die despite all the destruction that have been made to my body. His love only seems to grow as the day pasts.

Alessandra also came by today. For the first time ever, I saw hatred in my sister's eyes. But the hatred had not been directed towards me but the child that laid protected inside of me. She had told me that I shouldn't keep the child but to abort the child.

I refused her advice.

No matter what had been done, this child had been innocent through everything. It had caused no harm to me, only the man who donated the sperm. That's all he is to the child. A sperm donor.

Antonio, is the real father.

I already feel protective over this baby. Nothing will happen to my child under my watch. I will die before I let another harm my child. It's true what they say. A mother cannot love anyone more than their child.

~Isabella Valldarri

It has been a while since I have written in here.

Five months to be exact.

I've recovered from my trauma. Everything that Lorenzo have done to me has been talked out. I told them everything that had happened. Everything single touch, every single word, they know of it all. I felt relieved after letting it all out.

I felt free.

I am now five months pregnant with my little piccola. Yes. It's a girl. A beautiful baby girl that will look like me and nothing like the man who had injured us both. She will grow up, loved, and she will never know the truth behind her birth.

Antonio have gotten more protective now that I'm with child. He does not let me do anything on my own anymore. He cares about the child and talks to her every single morning. We have it all figured out.

I wished everything single day that the child is not only Antonio's daughter in name but also in blood. Fate is so cruel to us. If she had been his child by blood, everything would be perfect. I know it hurts him but I also know he won't love this child any less.

How did I ever get so lucky to get a man like Antonio? There is no better man that a man who fathers another man's child.

Hopefully, when my little piccola grows up, she will find a man like Antonio. A man who will love her even if she were to carry another man's child. Hopefully she will find a man who will love that child like its his own.

~Isabella Valldarri

.

.

.

The day is nearing.

Our little piccola will be coming soon.

Antonio and I are very excited.

He wants to be able to hold her in his arms and tell her how much he loves her. He promised me that he'll love her no matter what happens and I know I could trust him with her if anything were to ever happen to me.

I could tell that he will spoil her rotten. He will make sure that she is loved every single day and he will make sure that no one will ever hurt her as I have been hurt. I am proud to have a husband like Antonio.

I love him and even in death, I will continue to love him.

~Isabella Valldarri

.

.

.

Ashley closed the notebook back up and laid her head back on the pillow. She closed her eyes and held the notebook close to her chest. Her father had loved another man's child. He cared for another man's child and made her his own.

A deep respect formed inside of her.

Her father had been a strong man.

How much it must have hurt him to stare at her every single day of his life, knowing that she is not fully his. How much it must of hurt him to see the features of that man on her. How much it must have hurt him to see that she was the reason why the love of his life is dead.

Ashley laughed to herself.

It's ironic how Antonio knew that she wasn't his child and raised her anyways. Yet Dante couldn't be the father to his own child because of his arrogance and ignorance.

She sees the true man in Dante now.

A man who is too scared of being committed so he took the first chance that he got to get out of this marriage.

She should have known that someone like him would not stay committed for too long. He had been given a chance to get out of the marriage and he took it, all while blaming her for the destruction of their marriage.

She realized now that Dante never loved her no matter how much he had told her and even himself that he did. Love is about making sacrifices. It's about putting the person you love before yourself. It's about enduring years of hurt and pain just to do right by your love.

What her mother and Antonio had.

That had been love.

A love so strong that they fought against all odds. Even through death, Antonio still loved her mother. He continues to show his love every single day of his life. He loved her so much that he fathered a child that had not been his but yet still loved her as if she had been.

Ashley understood now why he had sent her away to be with her grandparents. It had been too much for him at the time. But she knew that he had never stopped loving her and seeing her as his daughter.

As his little girl.

Ashley got off her bed and limped towards the window. She grabbed onto the rails and stared down into the garden below. She smiled, seeing a heavily pregnant woman walking with a man. The man reached down and kissed the woman on the lips.

Ashley turned away from them, wishing that she had someone like that man with her.

At least she still had her family.

A family that she knew would never abandon her ever again. A family that would protect her and her baby girl no matter what happens. She know they've wrong her in the past but they were still family. She know how much they've changed.

Especially Samuel.

And she knew that deep inside Alessandra, there is a woman who still cared. A woman who is too afraid to show weakness but will do anything for the ones she loved. But Alessandra is too blinded by hatred.

"You should be resting right now." a familiar voice claimed.

Ashley jumped and turned her head towards the door. She smiled weakly at him. "Good morning Dr. Morcelli."

He raised his eyebrows up at her and crossed his arm over his chest. "Good morning Ashley." He walked over to her and reached his hand out to her.

She grabbed it and allowed him to help her back to her bed. Laying down on it, she smiled at him. "Thank you."

"You're welcome." He opened up her file and looked down at it. "How are you feeling this morning?"

"I'd get pains every now and then." she responded truthfully.

He nodded his head at her again. He sat down on the chair next to her bed and looked at her. "I'd like to keep you here with me until you give birth."

She gave him a confused look. "Is there something wrong? I thought I had been cleared to leave tomorrow."

He stayed silent for a few seconds. Those few seconds increased the worry inside of her. "I just want to make sure everything goes good for you. Keeping you here will let me keep a better eye on you."

"That's not the reason." she whispered. She placed her hand on her stomach, "Is there something wrong with my baby?"

He looked away, a sigh leaving his lips. She got her answer but he continued to lie to her. "No, there's nothing wrong."

"Please just tell me. I deserve the right to know." She begged him.

He looked back at her. He placed his hand on hers. "Do you trust me?"

She stared back at him, not knowing how to answer that. She had only known him for three days at the most.

Yet he just asked her if she trusted him.

Confusion swirled inside of her mind. She looked down at her stomach and noticed how big his hand was compared to her. For some reason, it felt like his hand belonged there. Right on top of hers. She didn't know why, but seeing that gave her the answer.

"Yes." she whisperd. She looked back into his eyes. Eyes that captivated her, drowning her in its deep. "I do."

He smiled at her and caressed her hand softly. "Then trust me that this is for the best for you. Trust me that you'll be okay. I will make sure nothing happens to you or your child. Both of you will be safe with me."

Ashley smiled back at him. "Thank you."

"Of course." he said softly, removing his hand away. He stood up, a faraway look in his eyes. He looked as if he was having a debate with himself before he shook his head. He smiled down at her.

Ashley noticed how fake it seemed. Although he was not a man of smiles, Ashley had seen them many times before. And she knew his fake ones from his real ones. "What's wrong?" she asked him. She grabbed his wrist.

He shook his head and gently peeled her fingers away. He held her fingers for a few seconds before releasing them. "Get some rest." he said, walking towards the door.

"Wait." she blurted out.

He turned back around. "Do you need something?"

"Can I just go home? Just for the week. One week wouldn't make much of a difference right?"

She asked, fiddling with her finger.

.

.

.

Alessio frowned. "I'm not sure if that's a good idea." His heart dropped in his chest when he saw the hope leave her eyes. He sighed and closed his eyes, praying that his decision wouldn't harm her too much. "Alright. But just for five days."

A smile made its way to her lips again and Alessio fought the urge to walk back to her and kiss those plump lips of her. He shouldn't be feeling this way to her. She's his patient. It's against the rules. Also, he'd only known her for a few days.

He scolded himself for being so hormonal. But with one look at her, he became putty in her hands. He didn't know what this meant, all he knew was that he didn't like it. He felt weak, and weak had been a feeling that he didn't allow himself to feel.

"Thank you." she said with bright eyes. "I'll be careful. I promise."

Alessio sighed and smiled back at her nonetheless. "I'll get your papers ready."

With that, he turned around and left her room. His legs itched to go back into her room and pull her into his arms. But he knew he couldn't do it. That would be so wrong on so many levels. But one reason stood out from all the rest.

He didn't want to overwhelm her.

There had been a strong urge inside of him to protect her ever since he laid eyes on her. The urge to make sure she never gets hurt and make her as happy as she could be. But he knew that he could never be that person. He would never be able to make her happy.

She is better off without him.

But for some strange reason, he couldn't help but keep coming back to her. He couldn't stay away, no matter how hard he tried.

.

.

.

So this chapter had been a little bit choppy but oh wells. I'll go back and edit it later.

So...

#TeamDante

Or

#TeamAlessio

???

Write who you want Ashley to end up with. ;)

Love you all of my lovely owlers!

~Amber <3 <3 <3

Chapter 19

So this chapter is pretty light compared to the other ones. There's a major shift in character for in this chapter and maybe you'll notice it, maybe you won't.

For those who don't remember, Frankie is Ashley's cousin. Just to clear up any confusion before I start on this chapter. ((: I am hoping to finish this book before the end of August but I guess we'll never know.

Hope you guys enjoy this chapter.

.

.

.

Chapter 19

A little boy walked up the stairs.

In his left hand, he carried a beaten teddy bear that he had ever since birth while his right clutched onto the banister. His little slippers squeaked with every step that he took up the chairs. With his eyes downcast, watching his feet to avoid any more accidents.

The yellings got louder. Every step that he took amplified what had been going on in the house for the past five hours. They didn't seem to be going away any time soon if anything, it kept getting worse and worse.

The boy stopped and closed his eyes. He dropped the bear and it tumbled down the stairs. He covered both of his ears with his hands and sat down on the steps. He shook his head, tears dripping down his face with every sound.

"Momma." He whimpered. He hugged his knees to his chest and began to rock his body back and forth. His body yearned for someone to wrap their arms around him and tell him everything will be okay. But there is no one.

A door slammed open and then everything became silent, a sound that became louder than that of the two yelling voices. Everything became calm again but he knew. There is always a calm before the storm.

The little boy uncovered his ears. He stood up and stared up into the third floor.

A woman came out of the door, looking down at the ground. Fear crept into his body seeing red blotches on the white silk dress of the woman. Her hair seemed as though it hadn't been washed or brushed in three days and her eyes had big bags lining up.

She looked down at him.

"Momma?" he whispered.

She smiled at him but there had been nothing warm about that smile. She looked like a snake, ready to jump at an unsuspecting mouse. Her tongue swiped across her lips and she sat down at the top of the stairs. "Come here baby. Momma needs to talk to you."

The boy shook his head and took a step backwards. His hands gripped the banister turning his knuckles white. "Where's papa?"

The woman laughed, throwing her head back. "Oh baby. You don't need to worry about papa anymore," she looked deep into his eyes, her lips curling up into a evil smile, "he's gone."

Tears dripped down the boy's face and fear crept into his body. He had never seen her this way before and it scared him. "Momma you're scaring me."

The woman took one step down. And then another. And then another. "You have nothing to be scared of sweetheart. Momma is here. Momma will protect you."

He shook his head again. "Where's papa? I want papa."

Her smile disappeared and in its place, laid an icy glare. "You do not need your papa." she smiled again. "All you need is me." she walked faster down the step.

He cried. "I want papa." he turned around and ran down the stairs, his heart beating in his chest. Halfway down, he lost his balance and banged his head on the edge.

"No." he heard a voice shout followed by a sound of a crying baby. "Sophia," he whispered before his eyes closed.

.

.

.

Alessio snapped himself out of the daydream as someone placed their hand on his shoulder. He turned around. His heart instantly pounded in his chest but he made sure to keep his face blank, clear of any emotions. "Ashley." he said, nodding.

Ashley smiled at him. The same beautiful smile that seems to always make his day better, even just by a little bit. She placed her hand back down at her side and studied him. Worry crossed over her face. "Dr. Morcelli—"

"Alessio." He cut in. He cleared his throat. "Alessio is fine."

She smiled again. "Well then Alessio."

He froze. There had been something about her saying his name that made him want to push her against the wall and have his wicked way with her. But he held himself back. Clenching his fist, he closed his eyes. He can't do anything with her. She already seemed like she is going through enough. He didn't need to add his problems onto her plate also.

His hand tingled. He opened his eyes and looked down at his hand, seeing hers holding onto it. He wanted to curl his fingers around but he didn't. He didn't do anything at all. He didn't even more her hand or pull his away. He looked back up at her face.

"Are you okay? You seem out of it." she asked him.

He nodded at her. It took everything in him to pull away. And with that action, he felt empty again. He cleared his throat. "Are you leaving?"

She nodded her head but then glared at him. "Don't change the subject mister. I know there is something wrong."

Alessio couldn't help but let a chuckle pass through his lips. Ashley looked like a fierce little cat, standing up to its owner but couldn't get her anger across due to how cute she was. He stopped himself. Did he just call her cute?

"There is nothing you need to worry about, belle." he said huskily. He saw lust passing through her eyes for a quick second before she masked it up. He smirked for a second before he too covered it up.

It keeps getting harder and harder to contain himself around her. She made him want to be better than the man who he became, better than the man who he only knows. She made him want to be better, just for her.

The thought of that scared him. He knew he couldn't change. Not even for her no matter how much he wanted to. The person he had become is too deep in the abyss to come out. He couldn't no matter how hard he tried.

He has to keep telling himself to stay away from her. To preserve everything good about her, he must stay away. He can't hurt her like he had hurt her.

Sophia.

His heart clenched in his chest just thinking about her. How all the light seemed to disappear from her eyes the last time he saw her. How the once bright girl that he knew had turned dark and hollow.

"Alessio, you're doing it again."

He looked back at Ashley, his eyebrows rising. "Doing what?

She frowned at him. "You keep going in this trance. It worries me. Are you sure everything is okay?"

He didn't know what he was doing when he reached a hand out and held her shoulder. He felt her muscles tensing under his touch but he ignored them. "Don't worry about me," he whispered, "I'm fine."

He pulled away from her and shoved his hands into the pockets of his scrubs. "I have to go now. I will see you in five days."

Ashley nodded her head and smiled at him again. "Will you be here or will Dr. Carson be here?"

"It doesn't matter. I'll be seeing you either way." He replied. He sent her his rare smiles and turned around.

Every step that he took away from her made him want to run back and pull her into his arms. But he held himself back.

This is what is best for her.

She doesn't need him in her life.

.

.

.

"There is something about you." Frankie commented as he walked towards her door. He leaned up against the frame and stared at her up and down. "Something seems really different."

Ashley raised her eyebrows up at him and continued to make her bed. "What do you mean? Nothing is different."

Frank shook his head and put his fingers to his chin, thinking. "No, you see your vibe has changed completely."

Ashley stopped what she was doing and sat down on her bed. She placed her hand on her stomach and rubbed it. "My vibe?" she questioned.

He nodded his head and then grinned. He walked into the room and leaned in front of her. "You met someone, didn't you?"

Ashley instantly blushed and shook her head. "A man? Me? Pregnant? A pregnant me meeting a man? You're kidding."

"Oh god you really did meet a man." Frankie exclaimed excitedly, sitting down on her bed next to her. He turned her towards him with a huge grin on his face. "Tell me, how hot was he? Chris Pratt hot or Colton Haynes hot?"

Ashley blushed even harder and slapped the backside of his head. "I didn't meet anyone. All I had at the hospital were doctors and nurses."

A light flashed through Frankie's face. "Oh? A hot doctor then?"

Ashley gasped and faced away from him. "Be quiet will you. You're disrupting my little one's sleep." she said, feeling a small kick towards her lower belly. One that hasn't seemed to happen until now.

"So it is a hot doctor!"

"You're annoying." Ashley muttered, standing up from her bed. "Why are you even in my room?" She turned to face him.

Frankie's face became serious and Ashley knew whatever he had to say, it wasn't good. "We have a dinner with the shareholders tonight."

Ashley raised her eyebrows up. She picked up a vase and started to rearrange the flowers in it. "Well what about it? Papi have the shareholders here for dinner often. What makes it so different this time?"

"Your father signed a contract earlier this week." Frankie started to explain.

Ashley then realized what was coming. She gripped onto the vase. "I think I know where you're going from there." She looked blankly into Frankie's eyes. "Dante is going to be there, isn't he?" she asked calmly though she felt none of that.

Frankie nodded his head. He walked over to her and pulled her into his chest. "Samuel, your father, and I tried to persuade the shareholders that it should just be us, but they want to meet the new lawyer."

Ashley leaned her head against his chest and shook her head. She pulled away from him. "Don't worry. I can deal with him."

Frankie looked at her with worry. "Are you sure you can? You don't have to go if you don't want to."

She shook her head and smiled weakly at him. Her hands pressed itself harder against her stomach. "No. It would make Papi look bad if I don't. I'll go. I will be handle him." she sighed. "Just promise me one thing."

Frankie gave her a questioning look. "What is it?"

Ashley grinned. "Don't try to hold Mayla back when she tries to attack him."

Frankie chuckled and pulled his arm over her shoulder. "I'm not going to even think about it. I think Samuel might even get a thrill or two out of it."

"There's something going on between them, isn't there?" she asked with a smile on her face. "There is no one other than me that can calm her down but clearly, she found someone else to do the job."

Frankie laughed and started to lead her down the stairs. "Mayla is a violent one still. Samuel has to put up with a lot if he goes for her."

"I'd appreciate it if you don't talk about my personal life behind my back, Valldarri."

Ashley and Frankie turned around. Frankie grinned at Samuel. "Oh come on. It's nothing you have to hide from famiglia."

Samuel rolled his eyes and walked down to where they stood. He looked at Ashley with worry in his eyes. "Listen it's your first day back at the hospital. You don't have to do this dinner. I don't want you to get stressed out and have harm come to the baby."

Ashley smiled and patted his shoulder. "I'll be fine. Believe me." She then faced the bottom of the stairs. "Trust me when I say, I'm over him now." she muttered, walking down the stairs.

"Of course you are because you found yourself a hot doctor." Frankie shouted, catching up to her even though it didn't take him too long.

Being pregnant made her slow and she had only taken six steps down before Frankie caught up with her in three seconds.

Ashley stood at the bottom and glared at him. She smacked his chest, blushing profusely. "Shut up about that."

"A hot doctor?" Mayla came out of nowhere, a smirk on her lips. "Does his name happen to be Ales—"

Ashley clamped her hand over Mayla's mouth. She glared at her family. "Leave me alone." she shouted, tears coming down her face.

A string of curses left Samuel's mouth. "Oh look at what you did, Frankie. You made a pregnant woman cry. Good job." Samuel pushed Frankie out of the way and pulled Ashley into his arms. "Come on, baby sis. Let it all out."

"You're a shame." Mayla muttered to Frankie.

"I didn't think she was going to cry." Frankie defended himself.

"She's pregnant and is highly emotional you idiot." Mayla shouted back, punching him acorss the chest.

"Well, you joined—ow!"

"I did nothing." Mayla stated before turning back to Ashley. "Ice-cream?" she asked with an innocent smile.

"I want a tub." Ashley hiccuped.

"Must be some hot doctor for her to not be a depressing little bitch any-more." Frankie muttered under his breath.

"Frankie, I will stab you in three seconds if you don't start being silent" Mayla warned.

"This is a violent family."

.

.

.

So...I have the ending planned out. AND THE ENDING HAD BEEN BASED ON WHO YOU GUYS VOTED FOR ON LAST CHAPTER. So if you didn't vote, you won't be blamed for how the book ends.

Now, some of you will strongly hate me at the end of this book and want to come after me with pitchforks while others would want to dedicate a holiday to me. Don't think you'll know how this will end but I'm positive that the ending will shock all of you. But that's okay right? Element of surprise ya know.

Anyways hope you guys enjoyed!

Love you all of my lovely owlers!

~Amber <3 <3 <3

Chapter 20

- -

This chapter is unedited. Actually all the chapters are unedited. HAHA. Anyways, please answer the question at the bottom. Your votes will determine how the book ends. ((:

Reminder: Elena had been Ashley's mother figure while she was growing up.

.

.

.

Chapter 20

Ashley felt a hand snake itself around her waist. A warm breath on her neck was all it took for her to realize who it was. She smiled and turned around. Leaning up, she pecked him on the lips. She held his arm with one hand and books in the other. "Good morning."

Dante grinned a her, one that made her feel as if the sun was shining on her back. "Good morning to you too." He grabbed her books out of her hand and intertwined his hand with hers. "How are you this fine morning."

"Good until you showed up." she teased, giving him a sly grin. They walked down the hall, towards her first class of the morning.

"I'm hurt, Ash. I thought you loved me." Dante exclaimed dramatically.

She rolled her eyes at him and punched his shoulder. "Who me? Love you? No thanks. I'd rather spend my love on dogs. At least they're loyal."

"Hey! I'm loyal." Dante stopped walked and pulled her closer to him. "Do you want me to show you how loyal I am?" he asked with a suggestive smirk.

Ashley huffed and pushed him away. She grabbed her books out of his hands and continued to walk. "Have your brain ever done any thinking or has it all been just your d*ck?"

"My brain thinks all of the time. It thinks mostly of you." he pulled her arm and turned her around. He smiled lovingly at her. "It thinks of how beautiful you are and how lucky I am to be able to call you my girlfriend."

Ashley blushed and looked down at the ground. She pushed him gently. "Three months and you're still as cheesy as ever."

"You love my cheesiness." Dante grinned and pecked her cheeks. He looked up and frowned. "We're at your class."

Ashley pulled away from him and sighed. "Finally. I can escape you. Your presence makes me want to shoot myself."

Dante scowled. "Hey."

Ashley laughed and kissed him. "I'll see you after class." she muttered against his lips. She pulled away from him and winked before opening the door. Walking in, Ashley had a big smile on her lips, one that would not fade for the rest of the day.

"Do you and Mayla want to sit with the boys and I today?" Dante asked her as she walked out of the classroom. He instantly grabbed her books and linked his hand with hers. "They want to meet the girl who had been able to tame me."

Ashley scoffed and pushed him. "Nobody could tame you even if they tried." She then became silent, looking ahead at all of the students walking out of their classrooms. Her steps became slower and slower.

"Hey what's wrong?" Dante asked, stopping her. He turned her around and looked at her with worry in his eyes.

She shook her head and smiled weakly at him. "Nothing." she said before resuming their walk. "I'll sit with you today. Mayla has to go meet up with her boyfriend anyways."

"Come on, there's something wrong. You know you can tell me anything." Dante said softly, squeezing her hand gently.

"It's nothing. Don't worry about it." she reassured him. She sent him a quick smile and leaned her head on his shoulder.

"It's not nothing if you look that stressed out."

"Drop it Dante. I don't want to talk about it." Ashley snapped. She pulled her hand away from him and walked into the cafeteria. She walked over to Dante's table without him and sat down, crossing her arm over her chest.

"Well who is this sexy lady I see?" one of the guys at the table leaned over and smirked at her. "Hello there sexy thing, what's your name? You can call me later." he said adding in a wink at the end.

Ashley looked at him and raised her eyebrow. "Not interested is my name." she said coldly, leaning back against her seat.

"That's what you get for trying to hit on my girlfriend, Nick." Ashley heard Dante say before he placed himself on the seat next to her. He put his arm over her shoulder as if showing that she is his.

Ashley rolled her eyes at his possessiveness. "Calm down will you." She muttered to him, seeing the glare that he directed towards Nick.

"Sorry, man." Nick replied, scratching the back of his head. "I didn't know that she's your girl." He turned back to Ashley and smiled at her, holding out his hand. "The name's Nick."

Ashley smiled him and shook his head. "Ashley." She elbowed Dante. "I'm this loser's girlfriend as he said earlier." She turned to the guy sitting next to Nick. "Hi."

He smiled at her. "Hi. My name's Thomas."

She smiled back at him. Already, she knew she was going to get along well with these boys. They just sent off the vibe that they were good people and did not seem to be looking for trouble. She turned to Dante and smiled at him.

Everything seems to be going just perfectly.

.

.

.

Ashley grabbed the first black dress that she could find and threw it over herself. She pushed the dress down, groaning when she saw how much the dress emphasized her belly. She sighed and grabbed a pair of flats out and put her feet through them.

She looked into the mirror and smiled at her appearance. She got to admit that the dress did some justice. Grabbing a red lipstick, she applied it on her lips and smacked them together. Feeling satisfied, she walked out of her bedroom door with one hand on her stomach.

Laughter and chatters could be heard down from the kitchen. It was pretty loud seeing that there is more than thirty people currently in her house. It's going to be a long night with them asking her father questions about the company and her about her pregnancy.

She sighed and walked down the stairs, holding tightly onto the banister to prevent any slips. Once she reached the bottom of the stairs, she sighed in relief and walked into the dining room with a smile on her lips.

Everything instantly became quiet when she walked in. She could feel everybody's stares on her. Smiling, she greeted them. "Good evening." she chirped cheerfully. She walked over to Antonio and kissed his cheek. "Good evening papa."

Antonio gave her an incredulous look as if not knowing who she was. "Good evening piccola?" he said somewhat questioning.

Ashley giggled. She looked around the table and spotted him sitting next to her father's worker, Rafael. She sent a quick smile to Rafael who beamed at her before sending a glare to Dante. She moved over to Samuel and sat down next to him.

"Someone looks different." Samuel stated, smiling proudly at her.

Ashley shrugged her shoulders. She turned to Mayla and winked at her. "I can't let him affect me anymore, Samuel." she whispered to him. She turned back to everyone else. "Is there something wrong?" she asked innocently.

They all shook their head. Elena smiled at her and stood up. She walked over to Ashley and placed her hand on her shoulders. "Some of you may not know her, but this is Ashley, Antonio's daughter."

Ashley smiled at them and stood up. "Hello, it is nice to meet all of you. Please enjoy your night here." She raised her glass of water and smiled.

They followed after her and clanked their glass against one another. Ashley sat back down and leaned into Samuel. "Why aren't you sitting with Mayla?"

"If I did, you'd be sitting next to either Frankie or Dante." Samuel responded, cutting up a piece of his steak.

"What's wrong with Frankie?" Ashley asked, raising her eyebrows up at him.

Samuel nudged his head towards Frankie's direction.

Ashley turned and saw Frankie playing the knife game. She cringed when she saw how dangerously close the knife got to his fingers. "Good point." she said, picking up her fork. She looked down at her dinner and grinned. Steak. Her favorite.

"How far along are you, dear?" a voice spoke up.

She inwardly groaned. Her steak would just have to wait for a little bit longer. She looked up and smiled at the wife of one of the shareholders. "Seven months ma'am."

The woman beamed happily. "Oh how wonderful. Your husband and you must be so happy to finally have a child running around the house."

Ashley felt a pang in her chest hearing that word.

No longer is she pregnant with two babies but only one. She looked down at her stomach. A tear slipped down her face and she hastily wiped it away.

She looked back up at them woman and smiled sadly. "Thank you ma'am but the father isn't in the picture."

She felt his stare on her but made no motion of acknowledging it. Ashley saw a flash of disgust flash through the woman's eyes.

"A child out of wedlock?" she asked with a hint of abhorrence.

Ashley raised her eyebrows up at her. "Does it matter, ma'am. What matters is that I love my child no matter when, where, or how it had been conceived."

The woman opened her mouth to respond but closed it as a maid walked into the room. "What do you want, maid?" The woman snapped at her.

The maid ignored the woman and looked at Antonio. "Excuse me, sir. But there is a man here, wanting to see Ashley."

Ashley stood up and gave her a questioning look. "Who?"

"Another one of her men probably?" Dante muttered lowly under his breath but Ashley heard it loud and clear.

The chair squeaked under the tiled floor. Ashley turned and saw Samuel's face red with anger, clenching his fist. Everyone stopped what they were doing and turned to Samuel. "You want to repeat that Hastings?"

"Samuel don't," Ashley warned him. She placed a hand on his shoulder and shook her head. "It's not worth it." she muttered to him. She turned to the maid and smiled at her. "Please, invite him in."

She looked back at Samuel and gave him a look. Samuel glared back at her and then at Dante before huffing and taking his seat again. He grabbed his fork and stabbed the steak murderously all while giving Dante his best glare.

Ashley rolled her eyes and moved away from the table. She looked towards the door and froze. "Alessio." she muttered, staring straight at the man who seemed to always send her heart into overdrive. "What are you doing here?"

He held out a journal and raised his eyebrows up at her. She looked at it closely and realized what it was. "Is this yours?"

Ashley nodded her head and instantly snatched it out of his hand.

"Who is that man?" someone whispered.

She turned around and saw everyone looking at her with shock in their eyes. Her eyes widened as she had forgotten that they were standing in the middle of the room. She grabbed Alessio's hand and dragged him out of the dining room area.

She pulled him out into the backyard and held the journal up. She smiled at him. "Thank you for this." She placed it back down and looked at it, seeing a few of the pages slightly out. "Did you?" she asked with fear.

"No. I didn't." Alessio answered her. He placed a finger under her chin and pulled her head up. "Reading that journal would be an invasion of your privacy. I respect you too much to do that to you." He muttered, before shoving his hand into his pockets.

Ashley took a step back and studied him. He wasn't in his scrubs but in black jeans and a white t-shirt. It was a look that she could never see Alessio in but yet he pulled it off as well as the scrubs. She bit down on her bottom lip and blamed her hormones for the many dirty thoughts that entered her brain.

"So is this him?"

Ashley and Alessio snapped their head towards the door. Ashley groaned when she saw who it was. "What do you want?" she hissed out.

.

.

.

Question of the chapter: If you could kill off one of the characters, who would it bc?

Dante?

Ashley?

Alessio?

Antonio?

Samuel?

Mayla?

Frankie?

Alessandra?

Choose carefully guys ;)

I love you all of my lovely owlers!

~Amber <3 <3 <3

Chapter 21

I kind of rushed through this chapter because I wanted to get it up for you guys. Finals are coming up for me so I have no idea when the next update will be. I estimate this book will be over in about 20 more chapters but I'm not entirely sure yet.

Anyways, I will actually post the first chapter of the spin-off once I'm done with finals. Also, many of your guesses of how Xavier is related to Alessio is totally...

.

.

.

.

INCORRECT! KEEP GUESSING YOU GUYS! THIS WILL BE VERY FUN FOR ME!

Anyways I hope you guys enjoy this chapter!

Chapter 21

Frankie raised his eyebrows up at her and smirked. He crossed his arms over his chest and ran his eyes up and down Alessio's body. Licking his lip, his eyes darkened. "Well, I must say cousin, you picked out a good one. Tall, dark, handsome, and very f*ckable might I add in."

"Frankie." Ashley hissed out. She turned to Alessio and smiled apologetically at him. "Please ignore him."

Alessio glanced over at Frankie before smiling down at Ashley. He turned back to Frankie and held out his hand. "My name is Alessio."

Frankie grinned and gave Ashley a side look. "I would take your hand but I heard pregnant women can be very possessive."

Alessio chuckled and pulled his hand back. "I have heard that a few times before." he said, grinning down at Ashley.

Her face grew thirty shades darker. She turned and glared at Frankie, motioning for him to get back inside the house.

He took the message and walked in. Before he closed the screen door behind him, he turned and sent a wink at Alessio while making the 'call me' motion. His laughter could still be hear even after the door closed.

Ashley sighed in relief and turned to Alessio. She blushed harder and looked down at her flats. She pushed a strand of hair behind her ear. Looking down at her journal in her hand, she stared at it as if it was the most interesting thing in the world.

"Your cousin is amusing." Alessio said smoothly.

Ashley looked up and smiled weakly at him. Embarrassment was all she felt in that moment. "He's," she paused, "Frankie."

Alessio chuckled for a few seconds before he put on his usual emotionless face. "Well, I have done what I needed to do here. I'll let you have dinner with you family in peace."

Ashley nodded her head. "I'll walk you out."

Alessio walked ahead of her and opened up the screen door. He waited for her to pass through before stepping in. "You have a lovely home."

"You don't have to be so formal. You're not Dr. Morcelli here." Ashley grinned at him, walking alongside him.

"Who I am here then?"

"Alessio. Just Alessio." Ashley responded. She stopped at the front door and smiled at him. "Thank you for giving me back my journal. I appreciate it a lot."

Alessio reached his hand out for a second before abruptly putting it back down. He nodded his head at her with a faraway look in his eyes. "Of course. I'll see you in five days."

Ashley forgot about the deal. She frowned and grabbed his wrist right as he was about to walk through the door. She ignored the feelings that bubbled in her stomach. "Alessio wait."

Alessio turned back around and raised his eyebrows up at her.

She removed her hand and placed her hand on her stomach. "Is there something wrong with Isabella?"

"Isabella?"

"My daughter." she whispered.

Alessio placed a hand on her shoulders. "Bella is fine. You're fine."

"Then why do I have to be at the hospital?" She questioned.

Alessio sighed and ran his hand through his hair. "It's for the best tesora. I want to monitor your stress level to prevent anything bad from happening to you or the little bambina."

Ashley closed her eyes at his choice of endearment. For some reason, Alessio always seemed to cease her worries with everything he says. But she knew that he is hiding something from her. Something crucial. "Alessio please."

"Trust me." he muttered.

A tear dripped down her face as she looked him in the eyes. "I do. I just. She's the only thing I have left to live for Alessio. Without her, I can't be anything. I would give up my life for her. Just let me know Alessio. So that I can prepare myself for the worse."

Ashley felt a hand on her shoulders.

"Ashley, is everything okay?" Mayla's voice said softly behind her.

Ashley nodded her head and wiped away her tears. She didn't remove her eyes away from Alessio's. "Everything is fine."

"Hello Dr. Morcelli, it's good to see you again."

"Likewise." Alessio said, nodding his head at Mayla. He looked at Ashley with a unknown look in his eyes. "I'll see you later."

Ashley nodded her head. "Thank you Alessio." she said, giving him a look saying that she's not done talking with him.

"Why don't you stay?"

Alessio and Ashley snapped their heads toward Mayla who grinned. Ashley had a horrified expression on her face at her best friend's suggestion while Alessio looked downright confused at the invitation.

"We have a lot of food and can use extra help in finishing it up." Mayla raised an eyebrow up at him. "Come help us."

Alessio shook his head with a tight-lipped smile. "It's alright. I must be getting back home. Maybe next time."

"Nonsense." she said, grabbing his hand and dragging him into the kitchen.

Ashley's mouth shot down. She hurried after them and walked into the kitchen feeling all eyes on her, Mayla, and Alessio. She looked at Alessio apologetically and mouthed an 'I'm sorry' to him.

He smiled back at her and nodded his head. He turned back to the crowd and placed his mask back on. "Good evening," he said smoothly without an emotions.

"Ashley, who is your friend?" Elena asked innocently.

Ashley coughed and pulled Alessio towards a chair, wanting the ground to open up and swallow her whole. "This is Alessio. He's my doctor." Her eyes moved over the many faces. She stopped when she got to Dante's.

His jaw had been clenched and his eyes narrowed. A vein stood out in his neck, throbbing. He looked back between Ashley and Alessio, his face getting redder by the second. He locked his eyes with Ashley.

She raised his eyebrow up at him and sat down. She removed her eyes from him and leaned in towards Alessio. "I'm sorry about this. I didn't know she was going to do that."

Alessio shook his head and patted her thigh.

Ashley shuddered at his rough yet smooth hands touching her.

"It's alright." he muttered.

It became silent. Nobody dared speak up.

Everyone had been staring at them for the past few minutes. They were the investigators while Ashley and Alessio were their suspects. All seemed to have the same thought running in this minds and Ashley knew exactly what they were asking themselves.

Is Alessio the father to Ashley's babies.

"Alessio, tell me about yourself." Her father had been the first to break the ice. He twirled his finger around his wine glass.

"I'm a doctor, sir." Alessio answered staring at her father straight in the eye.

Her father nodded in which Ashley hoped was an approving one. She stopped herself. Why would she want her father to approve of Alessio?

"For how long?"

"Ever since I was twenty."

"How old are you now?"

"Twenty-eight sir."

"Just two years older than my piccola." He said with a grin and a glint in his eyes. "Are you married Alessio?"

Ashley groaned. Even though Alessio didn't show it, she could tell that he is getting uncomfortable with her father's questions. "Papi." she glared at him.

Antonio raised his hands him. "I'm just getting to know him piccola. A man can't help but be curious."

"Unless he's a woman." Elena interjected, taking a sip of her wine. She winked over at Ashley. "Come on Antonio. Let the poor boy be."

"Let's talk business." Dante cut in, still glaring at Alessio.

"Actually, I would like to get to know this young man a little bit better. He might be perfect for my Carina." One of her father's partner said.

Ashley felt herself clenching her fist and glaring at the man. She grabbed a hold of her glass and gripped it tightly. She didn't know why but hearing the man say that about Alessio had her blood boiling. Could she possibly be falling for Alessio?

No she can't. There's no time for men.

She has a daughter to think of now and that is her priority. Also, men like Alessio does not deserve a woman like her. Broken and worthless.

"Any tighter and the glass might break." Alessio whispered into her ear.

Ashley shuddered, feeling his breath on her neck. She released her hold on the glass, turned and gave him a fake smile.

Alessio chuckled at her before turning to her father. "No sir, I am not."

Antonio raised his eyebrows up and leaned forward. "Do you plan on getting married Alessio?"

Alessio stayed silent for a few seconds. Ashley turned to him and saw his fists clenched underneath the table. She frowned.

"No sir. I don't."

"Why is that?" The man from earlier spoke up again.

Dante scoffed from across the table. "Men like him are not made to be a husband."

Ashley gasped and glared at Dante. She stood up but was instantly pushed down her seat. She looked over at Alessio who shook his head at her.

"Don't." he commanded her. He turned to Dante. "Do you have something against me?"

Dante raised his eyebrows up at him and stood up. He placed his palm flat on the table and stared at Alessio intently. "I do, actually."

Alessio leaned back against his seat. Ashley admired him for staying calm while Dante tried to get on his nerves. There were few men who could handle Dante's look. That was what made Dante good at his job. He sent the strongest men to his knee.

But Alessio seemed to have no problem dealing with Dante's look. He seemed almost amuse by it yet he didn't show it.

Dante seemed to also notice it as his jaw ticked and his fist clenched slightly.

"Please enlighten me." Alessio said smoothly. "Or are you just saying things because you think I'm here to take Ashley away from you? Let me tell you now, I have all the abilities to do that and I will if it means that she'll be happy."

Ashley gasped and looked towards Frankie who winked at her. She shook her head at him and turned back to the matter at hand. Dante seemed as if he couldn't get any more pissed than he already is.

"Gentlemen, please. This is a dinner." her father said. If she didn't know him, she would have thought that he meant what he said, but knowing her father, she knew he wanted them to continue on.

Dante looked at Alessio and then sat down. He continued to clench his fist and the vein on his neck throbbed harder.

Alessio turned his head towards Antonio again. " To answer your earlier question, sir, I am committed to being a doctor. Although I would love to be married one day, my line of work is not made for marriage life."

For some reason, Ashley felt as if there is more than what he is saying. She didn't press it though and sent a glare towards her father telling him to stop.

He didn't.

"Tell me Alessio, what do you think about a man fathering a child who is not his own?" Antonio took a sip of his wine.

Ashley's eyes widened and so did Elena's. Dante snapped his head towards Antonio with his jaw open.

Alessio, on the other hand, remained as passive as ever. "It takes a man to father his own child but it takes a real one to be a father to all." He gave Ashley a quick glance before turning back to Antonio.

Antonio grinned and tilted his glass towards Alessio. "I like you Alessio. There is something about you that belong in the business world."

Alessio cracked a smile but it was not like the ones that he had directed to Ashley. "So I've been told."

Ashley looked at Alessio. Truly looked at him. Her heart fluttered in her chest with what Alessio had said. There had been a desire in the things he told her father making there seem to more to Alessio that meets the eye. And Ashley is determined to uncrack every piece of him and see who he truly is.

As you can see, I gave up on the flashbacks. I'll probably go back and add one in for this chapter when I'm editing later.

Hope you guys enjoyed this chapter.

Love you all of my lovely owlers!

~Amber <3 <3 <3

Chapter 22

S o this chapter is a little rushed so sorry. Things are gonna get very heated up soon. Get ready you guys.

.

.

.

Chapter 22

Dinner went by quickly and silently after Alessio gave his answer. How can they say anything when he just sent most of these men and even woman to shame in under five minutes? He had been everything they weren't.

Ashley looked up him in the corner of her eyes.

He ate his food without making any kind of noise.

She couldn't even hear his fork scraping the bottom of the plate like she did with other people.

His movements were soft and graceful almost as if he had practiced them his entire life. Occasionally, he would look down at his food but his stare was directed to the wall opposite of him.

Everything about him in that moment stilled.

Despite how he managed to insult half of the men in the room, they admired him. They admired his honesty and his calmness.

He did not result to anger like Dante did nor did he subject himself to Dante's hate. He stood strong, tall, and proud. A man like him would have made it far in the world of business. No one would be able to undermine him and he would have all the shareholders on their knees.

Ashley finished whatever was left on her plate and placed down her utensils. She looked at her father, giving him a look that showed her displeasure with him. Crossing her arms over her chest she then turned to Mayla and focused her frustration on her.

Mayla smiled and shrugged a shoulder before bringing her spoon full of soup to her mouth. "It's rude to stare, Ash."

Ashley scoffed and rolled her eyes. She looked around the tables, her eyes landing back on Dante's face.

He's angry, she concluded. The angriest that she has ever seen him but unlike other times, he sits there, unmoving. He's trying to not make a scene anymore, knowing how Alessio will have the upper hand each and every single time.

Ashley smiled in amusement.

So the mighty Dante is finally beaten.

"What are you smiling at?" Alessio asked her.

She shook her head and turned to him. "It's nothing."

He raised his eyebrows up at her but said nothing. He only stood up. "Thank you for the meal, Mr. Valldarri, but I need to get going now. It was nice meeting all of you." He nodded at them and turned back to Ashley.

She got up from her seat also. Brushing her dress, she sent him her best smile. "I'll walk you out."

Alessio shook his head at her and placed his palm on her stomach. "It's alright Ashley. You should rest. The little one is going to need a lot of it."

Ashley shuddered slightly. Unknowingly, she placed her hand on top of his. "Come on. A little bit of walking won't kill me."

Alessio stiffened for a second. He walked forward with his hand on the small of her back. "Don't put you and kill in the same sentence ever again."

Ashley grinned at him as they walked towards the door. "Afraid to lose one of your patients, Dr. Morcelli?"

Alessio shook his head and opened the door. Ashley removed her hand. He shoved his fingers into his pockets. "No. Just you." He turned around and walked away. "I'll see you in five days, Ashley."

"See you." She whispered.

She closed the door and leaned up against it, closing her eyes.

Did Alessio just say that? How could he say something like that so casually and expect her not to feel anything towards it. He made her feel emotions that she hadn't felt in a long time.

Emotions that she wish she could bury forever.

She barely knew the man for a few days and yet she was already falling for him. Faster than she ever fell for anyone. He didn't have a reputation like

Dante did. Based on what she found out so far, Alessio has no significant history with the opposite sex.

He seems perfect but Ashley knows that he has a past. A past that probably is the reason why he does not want to get married.

She knows that if that past will harm her baby in any kind of way, she won't associate herself with him any longer. Her daughter's well-being comes first and will always come first.

Also, she doesn't want to stand around and wait for him to break her heart like Dante did. She's been through enough heartbreaks to last herself a lifetime. Another one would just kill her on the spot.

"You seem to be deep in thought." A voice said.

She opened her eyes and stared into the dark brown orbs of Rafael. She smiled at him even though she wanted to just walk away. "My thoughts are loud."

Rafael grinned at her and she couldn't help but feel a little uneasy. There was something in his grin that sent red flags all over her brain. "A penny for your thoughts?"

She shook her head and got off the door. "Maybe another day," she said, walking back towards the kitchen.

"I'll see you soon then Ashley," he promised.

Ashley heard the door open and then closed. She let out a sigh in relief. She never felt safe whenever Rafael was around.

But he was the son of her father's best friend and he served her father as best as he could. She couldn't do anything to complicate her father's life even more. Plus, Rafael wouldn't do anything to her. He had no reason to.

But she couldn't help but feel like Rafael is planning something. Something bad.

She shuddered and rubbed her hand over her stomach. She just pray to god that her baby will come out safe and sound. She felt a kick and laughed. "You're going to be a football player when you grow up aren't you?"

Another kick from Isabella as if she was agreeing with what Ashley said. Ashley laughed again and grinned. "Are you going to let me rest tonight?" she felt another kick. "I guess not."

She walked back into the dining room and sat down next to Samuel. Sighing, she leaned her head on his shoulders.

He wrapped an arm around her shoulder and moved it up and down. "Tired sis?"

"My baby is using me as a ball." she joked, sitting up again.

Samuel chuckled and looked over at Mayla. He winked at her. "When are we getting one, May?"

Mayla scoffed and threw her napkin at him. "In your dreams." she said with a blush on her cheeks.

"You'll definitely be in my dreams." he winked at her again.

"You have a very interesting family, Antonio." the man who wanted to arrange his daughter with Alessio said.

Antonio smiled at him and Ashley noticed how fake it was. "Thank you very much, Enzo. Your family is amazing also based on my past experiences with them." A glint in his eyes told Ashley how unfortunate the time had been.

She stifled a laugh at Enzo's eyes lighting up.

The poor man seemed to not be able to read people and emotions well.

She took a look at Frankie and bursted out laughing along with him. Feeling the urge to pee, she wiped the tears of laughter away and got up. She walked towards the bathroom and opened the door.

Walking in, she did her business. As she washed her hand, she stared into the mirror. The woman that stared back at her is different now. She had a light in her eyes again and there was more color to her cheeks. She looks almost, happy.

With a grin on her face, she dried her hands and walked out. Not looking where she was going to she bumped into the wall. Only, the walls couldn't move and it didn't have arms to steady her up.

She looked and frowned when she saw who it was. "Dante." she said coldly.

"Ashley." he let go of her as if she was poison.

It didn't hurt her as much as it would have three months earlier. In fact, she only felt contempt with his touch.

She moved around him but he didn't let her. He stood in front of her with dark eyes. "We need to talk."

She sighed and looked at him, exhausted. "We have nothing to talk about Dante. Everything needed to be said had been said during our divorce. Now excuse me, I need to go rest." She walked around him but didn't get very far.

His hand wrapped around her wrist and turned her around. He tightened his grip.

Ashley winced and tried to pull her arm away. "You're hurting me." she whimpered.

He tightened his grip. "Is he your new toy?"

"Let me go Dante." She whimpered, trying to move her arm away from him.

"Answer me, dammit!"

She stopped moving and glared at him. Her other hand reached up and slapped him across his face. "So what if he is? What does it matter to you? We're divorced Dante. Whatever I do with anyone does not concern you."

"It does if you're carrying my child." he released her hand and grabbed his cheek. His cheeks reddened and grew angry.

Ashley laughed humorlessly. "So now you think Isabella is your daughter? After everything, now you want to be her father?" her voice started to get lower and lower.

"There might be a possibility." Dante glared. "And if she is, I'm taking her with me. No child of mine will be with a mother like you."

Anger coursed inside of Ashley.

He thinks he can take her daughter away from her? How dare he comes and think he has the power to do that? After everything he said about her daughter, calling her a 'bastard child' and now claiming to take her away? How dare he spit out such bullsh*t.

She stabbed his chest with her finger. "You want to take my daughter away from me? I may not be a lawyer, Dante, but I know how the legal system works. You signed away your parental rights. You can't get them back. No court or judge will grant you custody over my daughter."

"I don't need a court or judge to back me up." he said coldly. "If she is my daughter, I'm taking her away from you, no matter what actions must be taken. Not everything needs to be legal."

Ashley felt tears dripping down her face. But it was not in sadness but in anger. "You're never going to take her away from me. She's mine." she shouted.

Like so many times before, her vision began to get darker. It happened so many times before that she knew it like the back of her hand. Her hand reached out and grabbed the closest thing to her. That had been Dante's arm. Her body swayed.

"Ashley?" His tone had changed completely. No longer is it filled with anger but with worry. "What's wrong? Hey, look at me."

She shook her head and felt herself being picked up by him. She tried to fight him but couldn't as her vision became dark and emptiness surrounded her.

.

.

.

"The pictures are real."

Thomas's body stiffened. He turned to his private investigator and stood up with his palms flat on his desk. "What do you mean they're real? They can't be."

The PI nodded his head and handed him the file. "I double checked everything. The images are real. There's no signs of photoshop in them or anything."

"How can this be?" Thomas whispered.

The PI shrugged his shoulders and stood up. "The file contains everything you need to know. I have a feeling this won't be over any time soon."

"What do you mean?"

"The guy you told me about. He's starting his plan now."

Thomas looked at the PI and placed the file on his desk. "Stop him before he does any harm to them." he ordered.

The PI nodded his head. "I'm on it."

"Also," Thomas started. He looked the PI dead in the eyes. "You can't tell anyone about this. We have to be careful or else everything will come tumbling down."

The PI paused. "I have a friend who might be able to help. He had been a part of the special forces."

Thomas sighed and sat down on his chair. "Contact him. Let him know we need his help."

"It might take a while to convince him."

Thomas glared at him. "Do what you have to do. Money won't be a problem."

The PI nodded his head. "Alright."

.

.

.

I swear to you guys, this will be the last time that Ashley will faint until she gives birth. But what happens next is so important that she has to.

Question of the chapter:

Who is your favorite character?

Remember that your answers do matter guys ;) Every question I ask will help determine the ending even if they're as lame as "what's your favorite color?"

Anywho, hope you guys enjoyed that chapter.

Love you all of my lovely owlers!

~Amber <3 <3 <3

Chapter 23

- -

I have another rant but I didn't want to make a separate chapter for it so I'll just do it on this chapter. Please read this. This is important and I need to address this more.

I want you guys to know that I fully support LGBT rights. I believe all of us have the right to be who we want to be and love who we want to love. No sick, twisted, or deranged person can take that away from us.

I think most of you have heard what happen last night in Florida. 50 people are dead in the worst shooting of United States history.

I felt so sick when I heard the news. Over 50 people are dead you guys. I can't even start to explain how I feel about this right now.

I just feel so sick and tired of seeing all the negative things that have been happening lately. First it was Christina Grimmie who was shot dead and now 50 other angels joined her. I can't believe how horrible this week had gone.

This needs to stop.

This hatred that brews in us. It needs to stop. We have to stop hating on other people and start loving them for who they are. This world is filled with so much destruction and violence because we made it this way. We're the only ones to blame for this.

Do not blame the religion, blame the sinner. Do not blame the country, blame the one who ruined it. Do not blame the world, blame yourself.

When I heard the news, two comments stood out to me the most.

"He had been a muslim. Why doesn't that surprise me?"

"I care about gays being killed of becausef?"

Those comments pissed the fck out of me because they showed no type of remorse or sorrow at all. None. They were filled with hate even if they sound so simple.

No, I don't think all muslims are terrorists. Some are the most kind hearted people that I have ever met. They are humble, kind, courageous, wonderful human beings who are wronged because of terrorists who call themselves muslims. BUT GUYS! BEING MUSLIM DOES NOT MAKE A PERSON A TERRORIST! Just as me being a Vietnamese does not make me a communist. Or being a Latino does not make a person a rapist. Or being a German does not make someone a Nazi. Please don't blame another person for the action of someone else.

No, I don't think that the LGBT community is full of sinners. What's so wrong about falling in love? What's so wrong about being with someone of the same sex? Did they rob you? Did they kill you? Did they hurt you in any single way? No. If they didn't anything wrong other than falling in love, how are they sinners?

We all have different religious and social beliefs. But that does not mean that it's justifiable for us to hate someone to the point of killing them. We all of the right to life. We all deserve to experience the good things in life.

No matter who you are, what you believe in, who you love, please remember. We all deserve to be happy.

Don't ruin the life of another person because you are not happy with who they turned out to be.

And for all of you out there who feel like you're misunderstood, remember that you're special. That you do matter. Don't let anyone take that away from you.

With that being said, enjoy this chapter.

.

.

.

Chapter 23

Dante caught her before she could fall.

She wiggled in his arms for a few seconds before becoming still.

Dante' eyes widened and he gently slapped her cheeks. "Ashley, come on. This isn't funny. Open your eyes."

Worry crept inside of his body and he made no move to stop it.

She didn't move. She laid limp in his arms. The only sign of life was the low inhales and exhales that kept decreasing by the minute.

Dante's heart raced in his chest as he stared down at her unmoving body. No. This can't be happening right now. She didn't just faint. She's going to wake up. She's going to be okay. But the rapid slowing of her heartbeat and breath proved something else.

"No." he whispered.

He ran to the kitchen with her in his arms. "Help me, please." he shouted to her brother and father.

A plate dropped to the ground, shattering and breaking into tiny pieces. Someone gasped while another dropped to the ground behind him.

"Ashley!" Samuel shouted, running over. He took Ashley into his arms and started shaking her slightly.

Dante felt cold and empty when Samuel pulled Ashley away from him. His hands fell to his side as Samuel tried to wake up Ashley.

"Don't just stand there! Someone call the ambulance."

"No time." Samuel hissed. "I'll take her. Come with me Mayla."

Dante watched as Samuel and Mayla ran out of the kitchen and out of the house. He stepped forward to follow them when a hand stopped him.

"Stop." A woman commanded him. Fury swam in her eyes and threatened to come out of her hands. "What did you do to my daughter?"

Dante shook his head, tears coming down his face. "I didn't mean to."

"What did you do to her?" Antonio spoke up for the first time. "What did you do to my daughter? You hurt her again!"

Dante shook his head again. He walked backwards until he hit a wall. Sliding down, he buried his head into his hands. "I-I don't know what happened."

For the first time, he's showing them weakness. For the first time, someone other than Ashley and his mother saw him at his most vulnerable state. For he didn't care. How could he care about how pathetic he looked when the love of his life could be in danger.

And the babies.

What if something happened to the babies?

He would never be able to forgive himself if something happened to the babies. Even if they weren't his, he knew that they were still innocent. Everything about them was still pure. He prayed that nothing will happen to the babies.

He felt himself being picked up by his collar. He looked up and met the furious eyes of a man. His face burned with rage and his eyes were dark with danger.

"What did you do to my cousin?" The man asked, landing a punch onto his face.

Dante pushed the man away and glared at him. Something possessed him and he pounced on the man, throwing a punch back. He straddled him and started to land punch after punch onto his face.

The man blocked every single one of them and flipped them over. He was quick with his moves, landing another punch to Dante's nose.

Blood dripped down Dante's nose as he pushed the man away and stood up. His hand held onto his nose that was probably broken. He looked at the man and noticed a cut on his jaw. Dante shook his head and looked around the room.

Disgust was the only thing that he saw in their eyes. He stepped back and looked into the eyes of the man.

Hatred and fury burned in them.

Those eyes scarred Dante's heart because those were the same eyes that stared back at him only an hour before. Only they were the eyes of a different person.

"I'm sorry." Dante muttered before running away.

He got into his car and shoved his keys into the ignition. He stepped on the acceleration and sped down the streets, not looking back once. His hands gripped on the wheel tightly and his brain replayed today's events over and over in his mind.

He didn't realize it until he got there and parked the car. He ran into the building, heading straight for the receptionist's desk. He was out of breath when he got there but he wasted no time. "Ashley Hastings." he huffed out.

The receptionist gave him a weird look before typing on the computer. She frowned at him and shook her head. "Sorry, I don't have any Ashley Hastings in here."

Dante stood up straighter and he looked down at his left ring finger. There was nothing on it. He had to remember that he are divorced now.

"Ashley Denorro." He gulped the ball that suffocated him. His heart beat painfully in his chest at the thought of the worse thing that could happen to Ashley.

The receptionist nodded her head and smiled at him sadly. "I'm sorry but only family are allowed in." She saw the heartbroken look on his face and sighed. "What's your name? I might be able to pull some strings."

"Dante Hastings," he paused, "her ex-husband."

He didn't know why but a scowl made its way onto her face. But then she smiled sweetly at him and pointed down the hall. "Third floor, fifth door on your right. It's an office. The doctor in there will brief you on everything."

Dante sighed in relief and thanked her. He ran towards the elevator and smashed the buttons. His foot tapped on the tiled floor as the elevator moved up. When it opened, he ran out of there and into the room that the receptionist had told him to go.

He opened the door and dashed in. The office had been empty. He paced around the room, wishing for the doctor would come in to talk to him already. He couldn't handle the anticipation any longer. He needs to know if Ashley is okay or not.

His phone vibrated in his pockets. He pulled it out and answered it quickly. "Thomas, what did you find out?"

"It's real but before—"

Gone was the worry he had for Ashley and back came the hatred for her.

He knew it.

He knew those pictures were real. They all lied to him. Her whole family is full of manipulative people. He should have known better than to actually believe that she had been innocent. There's no part of her that is innocent.

"I knew it." he hissed out. "I knew she cheated."

"Listen to me first." Thomas demanded.

"Fine. But nothing is going to change my mind again. I shouldn't have come to Italy. This had been a mistake. I'm going to get on the first plane back. I don't want to be here any longer." Dante shouted into the phone.

"Just listen for once in your life." Thomas shouted back.

"What is there left?!"

Thomas inhaled. "The girl in the picture. It can't be Ashley and it's not. They hired an actress or something but whoever that girl in the picture is, it's not Ashley. "

Dante's heart dropped in his chest. The fury slowly left his body and worry came back. "What do you mean?"

"Mayla and Ashley were together the entire time. The timestamp of the picture does not match the timestamp of Ashley. Dante, the girl in the picture is not Ashley. Someone impersonated her." Thomas explained.

"So you mean to say," Dante swallowed the ball that began to form in his throat again. "That Ashley—"

"She's innocent. The child is yours. Dante, I'm sorry. You're on your own now. You made the mistake, now you have to fix it before it's too late," he paused, "actually I think it already it too late."

He then hung up.

Dante let out a sob and tears dripped down his face. He couldn't believe it. She's innocent. She had been innocent all along and he blamed her for everything. He staggered back at the remembrance of the words that he threw at her.

He called their children bastards and signed away his parental rights. He then threatened to take them away from her. What father would do that to his own children? How did this happen? How could he have allowed it to happen?

God, he's a horrible human being. Through all this time he blamed her and made her the bad guy when all along it had been him. He was the one to blame. He didn't trust her enough to dig deeper. He just accepted whatever was thrown at him.

She's right.

He is a coward. He ran away from their problems instead of trying to fix it. He never confronted her about it.

He didn't even think about it.

He saw a way out and he took it. And he will never regret anything more than the day he walked out of that door. The day he demanded for a divorce before trying to find out the truth.

Thomas is right. It's too late now. He had already done too much damage to their relationship. Everything that went wrong had been his fault. No one else's fault but his own. He is the only one to blame for this.

He vow to himself that the moment she wakes up, he's going to repent, hard. He's going to beg for her forgiveness and do whatever it takes for her to forgive him and left him back into her life. He will do anything for her to let back in and allow everything to return back to normal. They're going to be okay again.

Everything will change from this day forward. He know that it would be hard to gain her trust again but she loved him before. She can love him again. She will love him again. They can be a happy family.

Once she wakes up, everything will be okay again. He will make sure of it. No one will stand in their way ever again.

Someone cleared their throat. Dante wiped away all signs of his weakness and turned around.

His eyes met with that of the man who he didn't hate until this evening. "Dr. Morcelli." he hissed out.

The doctor looked at him, bored. "Mr. Hastings. How unlovely it is to see you again. Have a seat. We have much to discuss."

.

.

Samuel's phone went off. He took it out of his pocket and read the text. He looked up and saw Ashley smiling at him. He sighed.

"You need to stop scaring us like this Ash." Samuel said, brushing her hair back. He kissed her forehead and smiled at her. "We should just rent a room out for you."

Ashley smiled at him and looked down at her belly. "I'm just glad nothing happened to Isabella." A tear slipped down her face. "I don't know what I would do if she leaves me too."

Samuel and Mayla both shook their heads. "She won't. She's like her mother, a fighter." Mayla said, holding Ashley's hand. "You just have to believe in her."

"I do." Ashley whispered. She smiled at both of them. "Thank you guys. For being here for me in times like these. I don't know what I would do without you."

Samuel smiled sadly at her and gripped her hand tighter. "Don't worry about it. We're family. Family is always there for each other."

"Ohana means family and family—" Mayla started.

"Means no one gets left behind." Ashley finished with a grin on her face.

"Disney losers." Samuel muttered under his breath.

Ashley gasped and threw her pillow at him. "Get out of my room."

Samuel rolled his eyes and got off the chair. "Gladly."

"You can do better than him, May." Ashley joked.

Samuel flipped her off and laughed before walking out of her room. He closed the door behind him and placed a mask back on. He walked towards Morcelli's office. Without knocking, he came into the room.

A smirk came to his lips. "Did you start without me?"

.

.

.

I really hope you guys read my rant. Lemme know if you did. Comment, PM, it doesn't matter. I will respond to ALL comments that deals with my rant.

Love you all of my lovely owlers!

~Amber <3 <3 <3

Chapter 24

Hi guys! So here's another chapter. That's two days in a roll already guys. Let's see if I can keep this up. This book is going to start moving faster because I just want to be finished with it already.

Anyways I need a favor. If you guys know how to make a cover and can make me want for "Only a Surrogate" that would be fantastic. I want to be able to start that book soon but I need a cover for it first and I'm bad at making covers. So if you can please make me a cover. Send it to my email at Ambyluvsz@gmail.com. Thank you!

Anyways with that being said, enjoy this chapter.

Chapter 24

Dante stared back at the doctor, hate brewing inside of him. The presence of this man never failed to annoy him. It brought forth the painful thought of Ashley moving on with this man instead of coming back to him.

He knew he shouldn't be blaming Alessio but he does. Because Alessio is the only thing standing in between him and his happiness with Ashley. Ashley is not a problem. She will grow to love him again and her family will grow to accept her decision.

"I have nothing to say to you." Dante spoke, walking towards the door. All he wanted was talk to someone who could tell him about Ashley and he knew for a fact that Alessio was not that kind of person.

Alessio put a hand on his chest and pushed him back onto the chair. He stood over Dante, glaring down at him. "You may have nothing but my friend and I have a lot to say to you."

"Friend?"

Just as Dante said it, the door opened. In walked in the man who Dante knew would not let him off easily. He smirked. "Did you start without me?"

Alessio shook his head and walked over to his desk. He leaned up against it and crossed his arms over his chest. "Close the door, will you?"

Samuel chuckled with no humor. He closed the door and walked over to Alessio, leaning next to him. Samuel looked at Dante.

Fear crept into his body. He didn't know why but he knew these two men could destroy him and everything he has ever worked for. He didn't want to but these two men scared him. But he stood his ground because he knew he had to get through them before getting to Ashley.

"Now you see here, Dante." Samuel started, dragging the words out. "You have to understand, we didn't want to do this."

Dante's eyebrows furrowed. "Do what?"

"Be in the same room as you." Alessio said. "If I had a choice, I'd just send a bullet straight through your head and be done with it."

Dante froze at how casually Alessio said it. He said it as if he would not regret his decision and would feel no remorse. He said it as if he had done it before. What type of men were Ashley getting herself into.

"We want you to understand," Samuel walked around the desk and pulled out a file. "How many times Ashley have found her way into this hospital over the last five months that she has been here."

He threw the file onto Dante's lap. "Read it." he hissed out.

Dante gulped at what he could possibly find in the file. He knew anything in there could range from good to chaos. With shaking hands, he opened up the file and stared at the first page. Ashley's smiling face stared back at him.

But she wasn't really smiling. There was no light in her eyes. Her smile did not show the crease around her lips. She was smiling but wasn't. At least, it wasn't the smile that he came to know and love.

"Read it." Alessio demanded.

Dante shot a glare his way. "I will." He turned the page and he frowned when he saw the date. It was dated a full month after their divorce. She had fainted while shopping for baby clothes. Her father's bodyguards caught her before she could hit the ground.

He looked down at the reasoning and the graphs.

Stress had been the major cause of her fainting. She had been admitted for only four hours under the watch of Dr. Carson. Mother and children were all fine but under strict orders for bed rest.

Her second visit was just a month after that. She had abnormally bleeding and stomach pains. Once again, it had been due to her stress. But this time had been different from the first. Their children had been in danger the time and at risk for a miscarriage. She stayed for five days before Carson gave her the okay to leave.

Dante gulped and closed his eyes. He couldn't believe this. Within two months, she had two visits due to stress. And the second time, she was at risk to losing the babies. How could this happen?

He never blamed himself more for anything than this. All of this had been his fault. If he had listened to her, talked to her, they could have avoided this. They could be back in their house, as in love as ever.

But he messed up and here they are. Her in the hospital again and him regretting everything he has ever done and said to her.

"Keep reading. It gets even better."

A tear slipped down his eyes and he made no move to wipe it away. He turned the page again. This time, the words hit him like a hurricane.

Arabella May Denorro: Deceased May 20th 2016.

Dante's entire world froze and cracked. He shot out of his sheet and stared down at the paper, the words haunting him. His hand shook and he dropped the file. He fisted his mouth and shook his head, tears dripping down his face even more.

"No, no, no."

He looked up at Samuel and Alessio. Both had solemn look in their faces. "This isn't true." he shook his head.

Samuel looked away from him and nodded his head. "She lost one of the baby. That day killed her. She would have died if it weren't for," he turned to Alessio.

Samuel didn't need to say anything.

Dante knew who had saved her. He looked at Alessio and saw something that he didn't. He saw a man in Alessio. Someone who was ready to fight against all odds and protect those he care for.

"You know the worst part about all of this?" Samuel muttered.

Dante snapped his head back to him. "How could any of this get worse."

Samuel looked into his eyes and chuckled humorlessly. "They might not make it in the end."

Dante gulped. "What?" he whispered.

"Ashley and Isabella, your daughter. They're at a high chance of death right now." Alessio explained.

Dante dropped back down onto the chair and buried his face into his hands. He cried and shook his head. "This can't be happening." He looked up at Alessio. "She must be so scared right now."

Alessio shook his head and glared at Dante. "She doesn't know and you'll keep it that way. Telling her will only add more onto her stress. Stress that she doesn't need right now. It would destroy her if she finds out."

"She deserves the right to know." Dante stood up and glared back at Alessio. "It's our baby and it's her body.

"No. It's not your baby. It's hers and only hers." Samuel whispered. "And don't you think I don't know that? Do you know how much it pains me to lie to her like this? But I won't risk the life of the baby."

"The life of the baby?" Dante whispered back. He shook his head and shoved a finger at Samuel. "What about Ashley huh?!"

"You don't understand do you?" Alessio whispered. "The love of a mother is a strongest bond there is. You weren't there to see Ashley when she lost Arabella. You didn't witness her trying to kill herself after finding out about the miscarriage. You didn't see the strongest doctor in the country break down in desperation, trying to save her. You saw none of that. So you don't understand why we made the decisions we did."

"We can have another baby. Just save Ashley." Dante hissed.

"If we let the baby die, do you think she'll be able to live at all?" Samuel shouted at him. He rolled his eyes. "Of course you do. You think as long as you're in the picture, she's going to be fine."

Samuel shook his head and smirked. "News flash Hastings, you will never get with her ever again. She's not going to be fine with you."

Dante closed his eyes. Samuel is right. She's not going to be fine with him but he's willing to do whatever it takes to get her back into his arms. "I know but that doesn't mean that I'm not going to fight."

Alessio stared at him. "Do whatever you want to do but if you stress out my patient and cause her harm in any way, shape, or form," he stood in front of Dante and glared into his eyes, "I send that bullet through your f*cking head."

Alessio stepped back and nodded at Samuel. "I will go check on her. It's ideal that we start moving her in now and not wait until the five days is up."

Samuel nodded his head back at him, both of them acting as though Dante is not in the room. "I agree with you. I don't want any more accidents from happening."

Samuel shot Dante and look before both he and Alessio walked out of the room.

.

"Are you alright?" Alessio asked her, sitting down next to her on the bed.

Ashley nodded her head and cracked a smile. "We have to stop interacting like this, don't we? I'm sure you're tired of seeing my face in this bed every single day."

Alessio chuckled and stood up. He face then became serious again. "I know we agreed on five days but circumstances have changed it."

Ashley sighed and looked down at her fingers. "I know."

Alessio sighed and brushed her hair back. "Listen, you're not a prisoner here. I will allow you to leave the vicinity once in awhile but I want you here to be able to monitor you. I want to make sure events such as tonight never happen again."

Ashley nodded her head and smiled at him. She grabbed his hand and held it, feeling sparks the moment she came into contact with him. Her heart sped up and she's grateful for not being hooked up to a machine. "Thank you for everything that you have done with me Alessio."

Alessio smiled back at him and placed his hand over hers. It didn't seem to bother him as much as it bothered her. But he was Alessio afterall. The only person he seemed to show any emotion around is her.

And she couldn't be more elated to know that.

"You can trust me to take good care of your and the little bambina." He placed his hand over her stomach.

She felt a pressure and smiled. "The baby seems to know who our savior is."

Alessio smiled although it did not reach his eyes. "I wouldn't be a saint enough to be a savior, Ashley."

"Babies have a way of knowing who's good or bad. I think you're a good man Alessio." She whispered, holding his hand.

Alessio smiled down at her and shook his head. "No, Ashley. I'm no angel. I'm not the good person you painted me out to be."

"You are though. You try to keep up this brave front but I can see through it Alessio." Ashley whispered.

Alessio closed his eyes and removed his hand away from her. He opened them again and Ashley saw them. Pain. Raw and strong pain in his eyes. They didn't seem as if they ever left him.

"I'm not the man you think I am Ashley. I don't want to ruin the image you have of me but please, don't settle for me." he whispered.

"Alessio."

"I know you feel something for me. And I admit, I do feel something for you too despite how short our time together had been. But you need to stop settling for less. Find the best guy for you." Alessio whispered.

"What if I just want you?" She asked him, staring straight into his eyes.

Alessio sighed. He leaned forward.

Ashley closed her eyes.

Seconds passed before she felt it. Something soft touching her forehead and staying there for a few seconds.

He pulled away from her and held her cheek.

"Alessio." she whispered.

"You deserve better than me." he whispered back at her. He stood up straight and then walked out of the room.

.

.

.

So question as before

#TeamDante

or

#TeamAlessio

or

#TeamIndependent

Or

#TeamNoOpinion

Love you all of my lovely owlers!

~Amber <3 <3 <3

Chapter 25

Definitely going to be editing this chapter later. this chapter makes me cringe...

Anyways, if you guys have covers for either Isabella or Only a Surrogate, please send them to be at ambyluvsz@gmail.com. I really need covers for "Only a Surrogate" though. So far I have a few but I would like so more for varieties ya know? Also when you send them, please include your wattpad name so I know who you are and give you credit for it.

Also a little shout-out to:

name_s_aphrodisiac

Sohazombie

EshaTheReader26

Twilightz6

Aye_Its_beba

Your guys' chain of comments really amused the heck out of me so this chapter is dedicated to you five! You guys can thank them! HAHA

Anyways, enjoy this chapter.

Chapter 25

Dante walked out of Alessio's office and towards the front desk of the unit. He cleared his throat to get the attention of the nurse working there. "Excuse me." He said with a hint of annoyance all because of that doctor.

The nurse moved her head away from her computer screen. He instantly recognized her. She was the nurse who dragged him out last time. Warmth were in her eyes before she recognized him and it turned cold. "How can I help you sir?"

"What is Ashley Denorro's room number?" He asked her, taking a step back.

"I'm sorry sir, but I can't disclose that information. You're not listed as her family nor are you on the visiting list." She said curtly. She turned her face back to the screen and began to type on it again, acting as if he wasn't even there.

Dante reached over and pressed on the power button, shutting it off. He shoved his hands into his pocket and glared at the woman. "Tell me where my wife's room is, now before you lose your job."

The woman looked at the computer, dumbstruck. She looked up at him, her eyes narrowing into slits. She stood up and grabbed the phone, pressing a button on it. "Security. Up to the fifth floor please. I need you to escort a man out for interfering with hospital policies."

Dante's jaw dropped open. The first time that she kicked him out, he had let it go. But this time, he won't leave without a fight. He reached over the desk and grabbed her wrist, digging his fingers into her skin.

"I won't repeat myself, where is my wife."

Pain flashed through her eyes but she covered it up and tried to remove her wrist out of his grasp. "Sir, I suggest you leave before the hospital press charges on you. It doesn't matter if you're a lawyer or not. Here in Italy, we do things a lot differently."

Dante's got to admit, this woman is stronger than most but she will fall. Just like everyone else. "Does it look like I care? Now, where is she? I will tear this whole f*cking hospital down if I have to just to find her. Or you can make this easy and just tell me where her room is at." he said through clenched teeth.

She opened her mouth but before anything could come out, her hand was snatched out of his grip.

Dante found himself being thrown at the wall. His back made contact with it and he groaned, feeling a sharp jab of pain on his lower spine. He stood up straight at glared forward at the man who he could not grow to hate more.

.

.

.

Red filled Alessio's vision seeing Dante manhandling one of his employees. He marched over to the front desk, his hands already forming fists. Dante didn't even see him coming. Alessio made sure of it.

Years of work had perfected Alessio's walk and movement to silence. And he used it to his advantage every single time. It's better to have the upper-hand by being silent. No one can ever anticipate the next move.

Alessio grabbed Dante's shoulders with one hand, easily pushing him into the wall while his other hand released Dante's hold on the nurse. A groan was all it took for Alessio to know his goal had been completed.

He turned to the nurse and inspected her hand. Pale marks stared back at him, slowing becoming red. It was going to leave a bruise, one that would take at least two days to fully heal. Alessio frowned at it. "Put some ice on it." He ordered her.

She nodded her head at him and glared at Dante before leaving.

Alessio looked around and noticed most of the employees have stopped working to stare at the commotion. "Get back to work." he barked at them.

They immediately looked away from the scene and got back to work. Some lingered behind for a bit but one look from Alessio and they all scurried away.

Another groan erupted.

Alessio turned back to Dante and walked over to him. He grabbed Dante by his collar and pushed him up against the wall. "Do not threaten my employees. I'm really tempted to send that bullet through your brain now."

Fear flashed through Dante's eyes and it stayed there. "I-I didn't do anything."

Alessio scowled at him and threw him on the ground. "You dare lay a hand on anyone, especially on my employees for no reason, you're going to get worse than just a little bruise on your back."

"I just want to see my wife." Dante stood up and brushed his clothes off.

"Ex-wife." Alessio corrected him and shook his head. "You're not seeing her. After the stunt you pulled today—"

"You're nothing but her doctor. You can't control who she can and can't see." Dante defended himself.

Alessio clenched his fist. He never liked to be interrupted. "Don't interrupt me when I'm speaking."

Dante glared at him. The fearful looking boy seems to be gone now. "Let me see my wife. We need closure."

Alessio chuckled humorlessly and crossed his arms over his chest. "Talk to her after she gives birth."

Dante shook his head and then looked down at the ground. "I might have to chance to do it if I wait. I have to let her know how sorry I am."

"That's not my problem." Alessio responded coldly.

A group of security guards walked out of the elevator and towards him. Alessio nodded his head at them. One of them saluted him. "Gentlemen." He said, shaking the hand of the leader of the unit.

"Dr. Morcelli." The guard looked around the area. "Who are we escorting out this time?"

Alessio looked over at Dante for a quick second and back at the guard. He shook his head. "I have it covered."

The guard looked at him unexpectedly. "Are you sure? We can handle whoever it is. All of my men are more than capable of that."

Alessio nodded his head. "Thank you but I have it under control now. Return back to your original posts."

"Yes sir." They all bellowed out before leaving.

Alessio didn't know why he didn't let the guards take Dante away. It would have made his life so much easier but something told him it wasn't right. He looked at Dante and studied him. Really studied him.

Gone was the cocky and self-absorbed man that he had met yesterday evening. Now in his place stands a man who wanted nothing more than the forgiveness of the woman who he had wronged. Something must have happened for him to change his mind like that.

Alessio thought back to their meeting in his office but dismissed that as the reason. Dante loved Ashley but he didn't love her enough to trust her. How could that be? What was a relationship without the trust? How can you claim that you love someone when you can't even find it in your heart to trust them?

Alessio wants to know the real reason why Dante is finally finding out his mistake. Before, he had seemed so convinced that Ashley had cheated and now all he wanted was her forgiveness. But what brought on this change of heart?

"Do you love her?" Alessio asked him, shoving his hands into his scrubs. He also regretted his decision.

"I do." Dante replied.

Alessio nodded his head. He turned his back around and started to walk away. "Room 521."

Alessio's heart broke in half and it pained him to walk away. All he wanted to do was turn around and land another punch on Dante's face but he couldn't do that. Dante is the father to Ashley's baby. He had more of a right to be there more than anyone else.

And he had the right to be a father to that child.

No matter how much Alessio wished it was him who was the father of the baby instead of Dante.

He didn't look behind him, fearing of what he could do if he does. He continued to walk forward and into the elevator. "Tell Dr. Morgan that she's in charge." Alessio said to a nurse that passed.

The nurse nodded his head and Alessio closed the elevator doors. He closed his eyes and leaned his head against the walls. He didn't want to think about her anymore. She had Dante now. But he couldn't help but think of all aspects of her. Her hair, eyes that always seem to stare down into his soul, and a body that made him want to pull her into his arms and never let go. He didn't want to think about her but he did.

The doors opened up and he walked out towards the parking lot. He got into his car and started his drive home.

The road were deserted. Nobody was in sight. Everything was empty. It was as if God was taunting him, telling him how the rest of his life is going to end up. He gripped the steering wheel harder and gritted his teeth.

He wanted to get rid of this feeling. The feeling of desertion and desire. He desired Ashley so much and wanted more than anything for her to be his. But he can't be. With the kind of past that he had, she would only get hurt in the end. And that is something that he refuses to do to her.

The only way to prevent her from getting hurt by his hands is to stay away from him. He need to keep every negative thing about himself away from her.

Alessio pulled up into his driveway and parked the car. He got out and walked straight through the door that was already opened for him. Taking off his doctor coat, he placed it on the hook and took off his shoes.

Little pitter patter of feet running across the tiled floor got louder and louder by the second. A laugh ran out through the halls.

He felt a body being thrown on top of his and arms wrapping around his neck. "Daddy!"

.

.

.

Ashley heard him before she saw him. She sat straighter on her bed and looked at Mayla. "Mayla," she whispered.

Mayla stood up and opened the door before he was able to knock on it. She looked back at Ashley who nodded her head. Mayla sighed and opened the door wider, permitting him to enter. She sent him a warning look, one that he did not seem to see before walking out of the room. "Call me if you need me or just page the nurses."

Ashley nodded her head at Mayla but didn't look at her. The only person she looked at was the one who was the reason behind all of her troubles. But she didn't want to cause any more trouble now. She sighed and turned away from him.

"What do you want now, Dante?"

He gulped. "I'm sorry." he whispered.

Ashley snapped her head towards him, shock covering her whole entire face. She had expected him to come and yell at her and threaten to take her baby away. But not once did the thought of him apologizing to her cross her mind.

Yet there he was, on the ground. Tears were rolling down his face and his head was down. Soft sobs could be heard coming from his mouth as he tried to hold them back. "Oh god I'm so sorry Ashley."

Ashley closed her eyes, feeling her own tears coming to the surface. She wrapped her arms around her stomach and shook her head. "No. Don't. Please don't. Anything but that." she whispered.

She didn't want to deal with this. She doesn't have the time to deal with her. No amount of apologies could ever make up for what he had done to her. He had broken her trust and broken his faith in her. Both of which can never be repaired ever again.

It was too late now.

"Arabella." she whispered.

Dante sobbed harder after hearing the name. "I'm so sorry. It's all my fault."

.

.

.

WOAH WHAT?! DADDY?!

You guys have to wait to see what I have planned out. Remember, not everything is what it seems.

I have a promise for you guys.

I promise to have Ashley be with the best person that she can be with.

When the ending comes, I will explain to you exactly why I chose that type of ending. For now, I have the ending finalized. But, you guys can always change my mind.

Love you all of my lovely owlers!

~Amber <3 <3 <3

Chapter 26

Fourth day in a row you guys! BOOM!

You guys get a little (a HUGE) insight on Alessio in this chapter.

Enjoy my lovelies.

Chapter 26

Alessio smiled and wrapped his arms around her little thighs. He did a quick spin. Her giggle echoed through the room, filling it with warmth. She replaced the loneliness inside of his heart with love. Full unconditional love for her. He placed her down on the ground and placed a hand on her cheek. "How's my little angel?"

She giggled and kissed his nose. "Good." she chirped. Her hands clapped together and her bounced her knee up and down. "Daddy, guess what?"

Alessio sat on the ground and pulled her into his arms. He kissed her forehead. "What is it, piccola?"

"I talked to momma and papa today." she whispered into his ear.

Alessio's heart tugged in his chest. He pulled her in for a hug, resting his chin on her little shoulders. A tear slipped down his face. "What did you, momma, and papa talk about?"

"We talked about you." she wrapped her tiny arms around his neck and leaned her head into his neck.

"What about me?" Alessio brushed his hands through her curly blonde locks.

"Momma wants you to get married, daddy. And papa wants you to bring a nice girl home to be my new mommy." she pulled away from him and clapped her hand together. An excited smile graced her face. "Are you going to get married daddy?"

Alessio smiled sadly and shook his head. "No, I'm not."

She frowned at him and stepped away. Crossing her arms over her chest, she glared at him. The exact same glare that her mother would give him every time he did something wrong. Like mother, like daughter.

"Why not?"

Alessio poked her nose and picked her up. He swung her on his shoulders knowing that she would forget about the subject.

Her giggles filled the room again. A sound of innocence that Alessio prayed she'd keep forever. He prayed that the line of work that he's in would never interfere with the life that she deserves. And that it would not kill her like it had killed Sophia.

"Daddy, put me down." she giggled, hitting his back with her tiny fists. "I'm dizzy."

Alessio chuckled and placed her down on the ground again. He held onto her as she got her balance back and ruffled her hair. "Alright piccola. You're down now."

She glared at him again and rolled her eyes. Her attitude reminded him every single day of Sophia. They had the same hair, same eyes, same smile. Their names were similar and so were their attitudes.

"Don't glare at me, Sophie," Alessio warned, "or else you're going to get wrinkles."

Sophie gasped and grabbed her face. She shook her head. "No, no wrinkles." she said in horrification.

Alessio nodded his head. "Yes wrinkles."

Sophie shook her head. "Nanna!" she shouted, running off.

Alessio chuckled at her and followed right behind.

She ran into the kitchen and hugged a woman's leg. "Nanna, daddy said i'm going to get wrinkles if I glare at him." she pouted.

The woman chuckled and knelt down next to her. She looked up at Alessio and smiled motherly. "You are home early for once Alessio."

Alessio shrugged his shoulders and leaned his body against the wall. "I didn't have much to do," he looked down at Sophie who stared up at the woman with widened eyes. He smiled at the sight, "I also missed my little piccola."

The woman shook her head and pulled Sophie away from her. "Why don't you go to your room for a bit? Your daddy and I need to talk."

Sophie looked at the woman and then at Alessio. "Will you play with me later, daddy?" she asked innocently.

Alessio nodded his head. She ran over to him and hugged his leg. "Do you promise?" she asked, holding up her pinky. Her big hazel eyes stared into his making it hard for him to say no. She had him wrapped around her little fingers ever since the day she was born.

Alessio smiled and hooked his pinky with hers. "I promise piccola."

"Will you play tea party with me?"

He cringed but nodded his head.

"Can I put a dress on you?"

His eyes twitched and he frowned but looking at the hopeful look on her face, he sighed. "Whatever you want to do, mi principessa."

She beamed at him and hugged his leg tightly. "I love you daddy." she shouted before running off towards her room.

Silence hung in the air after she left. Alessio shoved his hands into his pockets and sat down on the chair. He smiled in the woman's direction as she placed a cup of coffee down in front of him and then sat across.

She looked at him and smiled at the door. "Sophie is an amazing child." she whispered.

"I know Silvia." Alessio responded, taking a sip of the coffee.

"Sophia and Matteo must be so proud of her." Silvia whispered, looking down at her own cup of coffee. She looked up at Alessio. "You don't know how proud they are of you."

Alessio gripped the handle of his cup tighter. "Do we have to do this now, Silvia? It's been three years."

"Alessio," she warned him. "I know you didn't leave just because you missed her. You thought about them, didn't you?" she whispered.

Alessio shook his head and glared at his cup. "No, I didn't."

"Alessio—"

"Drop it Silvia." he hissed out at her.

She glared at him and leaned over, smacking him across his head. "Don't use that tone on me young man. I raised you."

Alessio sighed. "I'm sorry Silvia. I just don't want to talk about it right now. It's still fresh."

He closed his eyes and thought back to that day. The day where the only family member he had left was taken away cruelly from him. The day where he learned to close himself away from everyone else.

.

.

.

She held the bundle in her hand. Tears dripped down her face as the gunshots ran louder each time. She held the bundle up to her lips and kissed it. Her tears disappeared behind the layers of blankets.

Alessio got out of his car and stood next to her. He nodded at his driver before turning towards her. "Sophia," he whispered. One of his hand gripped a gun while holding out his other arm.

"Keep her safe, Alessio." She whispered.

She handled the bundle to him. Alessio looked down. Hazel eyes stared back at him, looking on in curiosity. His heart opened for the little girl. He looked back at her, his sister. Sophia. "Sophia, come with me. I can protect you too." he pleaded.

Sophia shook her head and looked down at her small bundle of joy. The tears ran down her face like a waterfall. She's never going to see her baby ever again. She won't be able to see her take her first step, speak her first word, or ride her first bike. She won't be there for the milestones in her daughter's life. Her first birthday, tenth, sixteenth, eighteenth, her prom night, her first date, her marriage, the birth of her child.

None of that.

Her daughter will have to go through all of that without her.

"I can't, Alessio. Wherever I am, she cannot be. She will be safe with you." she whispered.

Alessio looked down at the small girl again. Panic rose in him, seeing her face scrunch up and a tear slid down her face. It was as if she knew what was happening. He didn't know what to do. "Sophia, please." he whispered.

"Protect my daughter Alessio. Love her like she's your own. Let her know where she comes from but protect her innocence. Promise me Alessio." Her eyes held defeat. It was as if she knew her faith and accepted.

Nothing hurt him more than seeing her face like that. She was his little sister. He was suppose to protect her. "Sophia—"

"Promise me."

Alessio gulped and nodded his head. "I promised."

She smiled at him sadly. Reaching over, she kissed the baby on top of her head. The baby instantly stopped crying but reached her arm out to her. She didn't take her. She couldn't take her into her arms again because if she did, she would never be able to let her go.

"Please, keep her safe." she whispered before walking into the house through the backdoor.

Alessio stared at her retreating back.

"Sir, we have to go now." his driver informed him.

Alessio looked down at the baby. She didn't cry but it was as if she knew what had just happened. She looked back at Alessio and closed her eyes, a tear slipping down her face. Alessio leaned down and kissed her forehead.

He opened up the door and got in. He nodded his head at the driver and clutched the baby closer to his chest.

He looked at the house as they got to the front. His heart dropped in his chest seeing his little sister crying over the dead body of her husband. A man held a gun next to her head. One second, she was kneeling, the next, she collapsed on the ground.

His eyes widened as the blood spilled on the ground and his sister's head hit the hard ground. Her blonde curls laid in a mess being tainted by the blood that spilled from her head.

He wanted to stop the car and get out. Kill the man who had taken away everything he had. But he couldn't. Because if he did, he would break his promise to her.

And it was a promise that he would never break. Ever.

.

.

.

The memory was still clear in his mind. The day where he lost his only sister. The girl he swore to protect for the rest of his life. But she got hurt and died. And he witnessed it, not being able to do a single thing. He allowed the man who killed her to get away.

And he vowed to himself that he would find the man. No matter what happens, he will find the man and send that bullet straight through his head just like the man had done to Sophia. That man will not live to see daylight ever again.

The glass shattered in his hand. The blood dripped down but he took no notice of it. He didn't feel the pain of the glass piercing through his skin, but he felt the familiar clenching of his heart remembering her death.

"Alessio! Your hand!" Silvia shouted at him, grabbing it.

He didn't move. He just stared straight at the wall, empty. He lost his will to feel any kind of physical pain. No pain will ever be equal to the pain of losing his little sister. The girl who looked up to him and expected him to protect her.

"Oh god. You need to control that anger of yours. What if Sophie sees this? What would you say to her?" Silvia exclaimed, pulling the glass out of his hand.

Sophie. The only person he had left is Sophie. And he vows to protect her with every last beating heart. She will never know pain. He will kill anyone who ever tries to hurt her.

No matter what happens, she will be the only person he will ever truly love. She will be the only person that he would kill for. She is the sole reason for his existence and the only reason why he haven't given up completely.

She's the light of his life and without her, he would be stuck in a dark room with no sun to brighten up his day.

.

.

.

"Ashley please listen to me." Dante begged her. He knelt down on his knees.

Ashley looked at him. She didn't feel any emotion towards him. She didn't feel the heartbreak of having him in the same room, didn't feel the pity of seeing such a strong man result to begging. She was done feeling anything for him.

"If that is your way of begging for my forgiveness, you have another thing coming your way." she said coldly. She got up from her bed and pulled him up.

"Ashley, please. I don't know what else to do. I need you back into my life. I was wrong." Dante grabbed her hand and held it. "Isabella, she needs both of her parents."

Ashley ripped her hand away from his. She glared at him. "I don't need you in my life or in Isabella's. We're doing fine without you."

"A child needs both of her parents." Dante argued.

Ashley shook her head and smiled at him. "No, they don't. My father raised me on his own and I turned out just fine. Samuel lived with us but he mostly fended for himself, he turned out alright. A child needs nothing but love and support if not from their family than from themselves. I believe that my daughter will her fine without her father."

"Ashley please. We can get things back to the way they were before. Listen to me please," he whispered.

"Like how you listened to me?" she shook her head at him and smiled. "I learned one valuable lesson from you Dante."

He gave her a questioning look. "What is that?"

"I don't need a man who does not trust me in my life." she pointed towards the door before moving back to her bed. "You know the way out."

"Ashley—"

"I need my sleep, Dante. Please, show yourself the exit or I could get security in her again." she closed her eyes and laid down the pillow.

"Alright. But this isn't over. I will continue to fight for you." He said with conviction.

"That doesn't mean that we'll be together. I have made my decision Dante. And you do not come anywhere near it." she smiled and willed herself to sleep.

.

.

.

Wowow...

Hm...

Q1: What do you think about Sophia's death?

Q2: Do you love me or nawh? ;)

#TeamDante

#TeamAlessio

Remember to send me covers if possible for either "Isabella" or "Only a Surrogate" at ambyluvsz@gmail.com.

Love you all of my lovely owlers!

~Amber <3 <3 <3

~Amber <3 <3 <3

Chapter 27

So somethings I need to point out:

THIS STORY IS ENTIRELY FICTIONAL. Every single event is made up. With that being said, things may seem strange in this story and may not happen in real life but in this story, it happens so DEAL WITH IT!

Also, if you want to stop reading this then by all means, go ahead. But please don't write comments telling me that you're going to stop reading. In a way, it's a rude to me. It's saying that my writing isn't good enough for you to continue and it hurts. So please, I'm not forcing you to read this. If at any time, you decide this book isn't for you then stop reading it. All I ask is that you don't comment that you're going to stop reading.

I will also be starting "Only a Surrogate" next week.

This book will be coming to an end soon. Like ten more ish chapters.

WARNING: THIS CHAPTER IS A LITTLE BIT ON THE DARKER SIDE! SO PLEASE READ AT YOUR OWN RISK!

With that being said, I hope you guys enjoy this chapter.

.

.

.

Chapter 27

It has been three weeks since the last time that Ashley saw Dante. But yet, even though he was not there, he still made his presence known. Every single day, she would receive a bouquet of roses that the nurse would bring in at twelve sharp. The colors varied because Ashley believed all the colors were beautiful.

As nice as the gesture was to her, she still couldn't forget what he had done to her. Many times, he had been the reason why she had to go to the hospital. And he was the reason why she had lost Arabella.

She knew how much he wanted things to go back to the way it was but he was living an illusion. After everything that had happened, nothing could go back to the way it was. How could it when all of their trust and belief in each other flew away in just a snap of a finger. It would be nearly impossible to be able to build it all back it.

She smiled down at her stomach and caressed it. She did a lot of thinking though. Dante and her could never go back to the way it was but he was still Isabella's father. She sighed. She couldn't keep Dante away from Isabella. It would be cruel of her to take away her daughter's father.

Ashley knew she would be able to tolerate Dante and maybe they could even become friends but never would they get back to each other. Their relationship was far too damaged to be fixed. Getting back into it would be toxic not only for her but also for Isabella.

She didn't have time to think about herself anymore. She had a baby due in a month's time. Every single decision, regardless of how little it may seem, will not benefit her but her daughter. Her daughter is the only thing that matters to her in the world right now.

Ashley sighed. Her thoughts drifted towards Alessio. Also something else that has changed. She hadn't seen him in over three weeks. Lately, the doctor that checked up on her had been Dr. Morgan, a young doctor with a heart of gold.

As nice as Dr. Morgan was, Ashley couldn't help but miss Alessio. She knew she couldn't have him and she accepted it. But still, she couldn't help but feel a yearning towards him. She was the moth and he was her flame. A flame that seemed to only burn brighter and brighter with each passing day.

She wondered what had happened to him. Was he okay? Why did he leave without saying as much as good-bye to her? Did he have someone waiting for him on the side? Was everything he told her been just a lie?

No.

He had no obligation towards her. He wasn't her boyfriend and he definitely wasn't her husband. She had no right to question him.

"Good morning, beautiful."

Ashley looked up. Her eyes widened and she gulped. "Rafael. What a surprise to see you here. How are you?" she asked politely.

Rafael grinned and her and sat down on the chair. He grabbed her hand and kissed her knuckles. "I've been fine. How are you?"

Ashley hastily snatched her hand away from him, not missing the determined glint that passed through his eyes. She smiled at him, scooting a little further back. "I've been fine."

He raised his eyebrows up at her. He then stared down at her stomach before looking back up at her. Although he tried to mask it, Ashley could see the disgust that brewed in his eyes. "How is your little bambina?"

"Fine." Her fingers hovered over the red button, ready to press it.

Rafael had never done anything to harm her but something inside told her to stay away from him. Rafael was attractive no doubt about that but there was something sinister hiding in his eyes. Something that he tried to hide but Ashley saw right through it every single time.

She knew he was infatuated with her. She had known ever since they were little kids. Even looking at him now, she didn't miss the hopeful gleam in his eyes that only shined from time to time.

"I don't see any use for that button at all." Rafael hummed and stood up. He walked towards the door and closed it. Turning back, he smirked at her. "Why don't we have a little talk? There's so much for us to discuss."

Ashley's heart jumped out of her chest seeing the door closed. She pressed the button, hoping that he didn't notice it. "About what?"

He walked back to her and caressed her cheek. He grabbed her shoulders and buried his head into her neck. He breathed her in.

Goosebumps rose all over Ashley's skin. She breathed out slowly and unevenly. "Rafael?" she whispered, pushing him away.

He held her shoulders tighter. "You don't know how much I want you right now." he whispered into her ear, "how much I have always wanted you."

He moved her hand away from the button and chuckled. "That isn't going to help you. They won't know a thing. All the cameras are shut down and so are the alarms."

Ashley shivered and tried to push him away. "Rafael please."

He laughed again and placed a kiss on her neck. His tongue darted out and licked the spot beneath her ear. "I can taste you."

Ashley closed her eyes. A tear dripped down her face. She clenched her fist. "Rafael, please I'm begging you. Let me go."

He pulled away from her and smiled, His hand touched her cheek and pushed her down on the bed. His eyes darkened as he roamed all over her body. He pulled out a cuff.

Ashley pushed him off and stood up but he only pushed her back on the bed again. She tried to fight back but couldn't as he straddled her and cuffed her arms to the bed. He grabbed another one and cuffed her legs. She shook her head and begged him. "Why are you doing this?"

"I watched you. You married another man and now you're pregnant." he glared down at her and climbed on top again. "How could you?" he asked, grinding his hips against her core.

"No please, don't." Ashley begged him, her hand instinctively moving to her stomach. She opened her mouth and screamed when she realized that he wasn't going to go anywhere.

Rafael clasped his hand over her mouth and pushed down on it. He glared at her. "Your screams won't do anything, don't even try."

His other hand moved beneath her gown, touching her stomach. He grinned at her and grinded his hips on her lower region. "Can you feel how much I want you?" he whispered. "I want to hear you scream my name.

Whether it's in pleasure or pain. I just want to sweet sound of my name coming out of your mouth."

Ashley wiggled beneath him, her tears coming down faster. She begged for someone to come and save her.

"You know what I love most about private rooms? They're practically sound-proof." He groaned. His hands traced up her body.

She snapped her eyes shut and begged for him to remove his hands away from her. She didn't want to feel his touch. It made her feel dirty.

She gasped when pain coursed through her breasts. Her eyes snapped over and met Rafael's eyes. Eyes that were dark with evil.

He grinned at her and removed his hand away from her mouth. "I want to taste you." he whispered before laying kisses on her neck. He removed her gown.

Ashley screamed again.

He chuckled and his head disappeared from view.

She felt him. Felt his breath blowing over her. She tried to close her legs but the cuffs prevented her from doing anything. "Alessio!" she shouted, tears dripping down her face.

"He won't save you." Rafael whispered.

Her body twitched and she felt her insides clenching. She closed her eyes and prayed. Prayed for Alessio to come and save her. She prayed from this to be over. She prayed to forget Rafael's touch.

"Can you blame me for wanting you? Someone so beautiful and innocent? You're perfect to me." he whispered.

"Don't." she whispered. "Please, Rafael. Don't do this to me."

He groaned. "Your begging only make me want this more and more."

"Why?" Ashley felt hopeless laying on the bed, bare. She couldn't do anything. Not without inflicting more harm onto her baby.

Rafael moved away from her, standing across the room. He looked away with his fist clenched. "You never noticed me. You sought love when you could have been with me. We could have been in love with each other." he glared at her stomach. "That child could have been mine."

Ashley shook her head. "Please Rafael, let me go."

His throat rumbled. "You're mine, Ashley. No matter what happens, you're mine."

He looked at her longingly and turned around.

"Rafael no. Unlock me." she cried out as he walked out of the door. She wiggled again the cuffs, her eyes blurred with tears. "Rafael!"

A team of doctors and nurses must have heard her cries as they rushed into the room. They took once glance at her and looked at each other.

Ashley cried harder and wiggled around the chains harder. "Please get me out of these." she begged them.

"Find me Dr. Morcelli, now!" Dr. Morgan shouted.

She came over to Ashley's side and touched her gently. "We'll get you out of these, Ashley."

Ashley sobbed harder and she grabbed Dr. Morgan's arm. She held onto it tightly, thinking that if she was to let go, more harm would come her way.

Why did all bad things happen to her? Why?

Alessio picked up his phone. "Morcelli." he answered gruffly, shifting Sophie to his other arm while holding the phone in the other.

"Good afternoon Dr. Morcelli. My name is Thomas. I need your help on something quite important." A voice echoed through the phone.

Alessio sat down on his office chair and positioned Sophie's head on his shoulders. "How can I help you?"

"You were once part of the Special Forces, no?"

"That had been eight years ago." Alessio answered him coldly, already knowing where it was heading.

"Yes but you see, we need someone with skills much like yours." Thomas replied, not seeming the least bothered.

"I don't do anything with the Special Forces anymore."

"You don't need to. We just need your skills."

Alessio could hear the annoyance starting to seep through the man. He rolled his eyes. "Whatever it is, it will be a no."

"Not even when it comes to Ashley Valldarri?" His voice came out smug.

Alessio stood up from his seat, forgetting completely about Sophie. Sophie opened her eyes, and Alessio cursed himself. "Daddy?"

He held a finger to his lips, smiling and kissing her forehead when she nodded her head. She leaned her head against his shoulder, wrapping her arm around his neck. Alessio sighed. "What does Ashley have to do with this?"

"Protect her and keep an eye out on someone."

"Who?" Alessio's blood boiled at the thought of someone coming Ashley. He would kill anyone who dares to hurt her ever again.

"Rafael De Luca."

Alessio's chest rumbled. "Done." he snapped before shutting off his phone. He shoved it into his pocket and looked down at his sleeping baby girl. He pushed her hair back and kissed the top of her head. He walked of his office and towards her room.

Placing her down on the bed, he gently caressed her cheek. Her light snores filled up the room. Like mother like daughter the saying goes. He chuckled at her crinkling nose. She's perfect. Everything about her reminded him of his sister. The sister that he couldn't protect. The thought of it made his blood boil.

His phone vibrated in his pocket. He groaned and pulled his phone out, ignoring the pink coats on his fingernails. He would just have to clean them off later.

He opened his phone and when his eyes met the message on the screen, he felt his eyes burning with fury. Walking out of Sophie's room, he threw the phone across the hall. He ran down the stairs and grabbed his gun from his desk drawer.

"Silvia, watch Sophie." he shouted before running out into his car.

Someone had hurt Ashley and he wasn't there to stop it.

.

.

www.ingramcontent.com/pod-product-compliance
Lightning Source LLC
Chambersburg PA
CBHW071430200726
48294CB00002B/586